monsoonbooks

THE PHOENIX AND THE CROW

Graham Sage was born in England in 1948. He is a graduate of Strasbourg University, France, and Oxford University, UK, where he read Modern Languages. He is British by nationality and a Permanent Resident of Singapore, where he has lived and worked since 1974. Now retired, he spends his time travelling between Singapore, Chengdu, Phnom Penh and Strasbourg pursuing his passion for writing.

T0150032

THE PHOENIX
AND
THE CROW

GRAHAM SAGE

monsoon

monsoonbooks

First published in 2016
by Monsoon Books Ltd
www.monsoonbooks.com.sg

No.1 Duke of Windsor Suite, Burrough Court, Burrough on
the Hill, Leics. LE14 2QS, UK *and* 150 Orchard Road #07-02,
Singapore 238841.

First edition.

ISBN (paperback): 978-981-4625-41-8
ISBN (ebook): 978-981-4625-42-5

Cover design by Cover Kitchen.

Printed in Great Britain by Clays Ltd, St Ives plc
18 17 16   1 2 3 4 5

For the many poor people in the world
who have suffered at the hands
of corrupt people in power.

'We must uphold the fighting of tigers and flies ...'

Xi Jinping

1

Paintwork on the wooden window frame had flaked off in places and been rubbed clean. Patches of previous layers showed through. One section of the frame, where the window latch was, had been replaced and the plain wood left unpainted, barely sanded down. There was evidence of a new windowpane. Wang Bin wondered how the previous one had been broken.

He had taken a room in the government-owned Pingyang Merchants Hotel, off the main street running through the centre of town. The room was clean but not cosy. There were two single beds with wooden headboards and hard, fibre mattresses. The beds occupied most of the space in the room. There was also a desk and a chair, and an old TV set perched on top of a low empty cabinet where extra blankets might once have been kept.

A musty smell pervaded; made him suspect the room

was seldom occupied. Perhaps he should have taken a cheaper one, without air-conditioning, more in line with a local person's budget, more often used, its windows more often opened. This room looked neglected, unkempt, inhospitable. The veneer on the furniture was coming unstuck, the ceramic floor tiles cracked in several places, the bathroom bleak with its rusty metal shower-rose.

Tired though he was, he got up from where he was lying on one of the beds and went to take a closer look at the window. A newer screw had been used to secure the latch.

His room was on the ground floor and the view from the window looked directly into a space behind the hotel. Some cars were parked there. There were, too, a few scraggly saplings, irregularly, carelessly placed, trying to stay alive.

On the other side, beyond the cars, he could see the hotel kitchen, quiet at this hour of the day. The afternoon sun caught the grime around the windows, softened the streaks of soot higher up, made a halo around the place where a tin-tube chimney stuck out at an angle. The walls of the building, perhaps once white, were now the colour of pork fat set firm in a dirty frying pan, burnt bacon bits included.

The back door to the kitchen opened. One of the cooks stepped out, yawned, urinated against the wall and went back inside to continue his siesta.

Wang Bin's gaze travelled along the wall from the damp patch left by the cook to the section where the hotel reception area was located. Double doors with glass panes were wedged open. A covered walkway connected it to the building where his and all the other hotel rooms were. The other side of the reception building opened onto Pingyang's main street.

The air-conditioner in his room was beginning to do its job. Wang Bin went back to stretch out on the bed. He had chosen the one closer to the bathroom.

Pingyang was a small town nestled in the mountains between Sichuan and Hunan. It was not easily accessible and Wang Bin had spent a tiring day travelling by public bus over the single rough and dusty road, which linked the two provinces. The town was a long way from the administrative centres of both provinces and a long way down on their respective Public Works Department's budget for road repairs. Some people in Pingyang liked it that way. They reckoned the less interference from the provincial government, the better. Because of its location as a border town, it provided a good stopping off point for travelling salesmen and truck drivers to spend the night. It also acquired a certain notoriety for other night-time activities.

The mountains around Pingyang were covered in primitive forest, an ideal habitat for rare species of flora and fauna and a spiritual retreat for Taoist hermits. It was in these mountains that a certain rare bird was believed to exist. High on the endangered species list, it had been dubbed the 'Mountain Phoenix' by the Beijing Ornithological Society of which Wang Bin was a member. Similar in size and shape to its far more common cousin, the Mountain Heron (*ardea himalaya*), the Mountain Phoenix (*ardea magnificens imperatora*) dazzled anyone lucky enough to catch a glimpse of it, with a blaze of rich colours in its plumage, from the bright orange bib finely outlined in black, to the two scarlet plumes sweeping backwards from its head, to the turquoise and emerald spots on the tips of its tail feathers.

Every year Pingyang attracted a number of enthusiastic birdwatchers, mostly individuals like Wang Bin, keen to spot the rare species and catch it through a camera lens. None had so far been lucky enough to succeed. The bird was enticingly elusive. It had recently been the subject of renewed interest after *International Birdwatcher's Digest* had published an article on the famous explorer and sinologist, Ben Hadlock, and his travels in this part of China. The article described the bird in detail, together with other rare and perhaps now extinct species. There was even a coloured drawing of the Mountain Phoenix done by Hadlock himself. Wang Bin was here now to try to find the bird and take some photographs of it. If he succeeded he would become famous within the society.

Wang Bin dreamed of breaking into the society's inner circle. It was full of stuffy, conservative old men who still condoned Mao's drive to purge China of the sparrow. Some had even participated in the banging of pots and pans to keep the little birds airborne until they succumbed to exhaustion and dropped to the ground. Death by percussion.

He knew the members of the inner circle disliked him. His enthusiasm. His regularly rejected suggestions to improve everything within the society. His drive for internationalisation.

That is why he had not told anyone of his holiday plans this year, to walk in the footsteps of Ben Hadlock, in pursuit of the Mountain Phoenix.

He would show them.

He might even get his photos published in *International Birdwatcher's Digest*. The Beijing Ornithological Society would at last have to recognize him. They might even put up a plaque in their meeting hall with his name inscribed on it.

He had inadvertently left the door to his room unlocked from the inside and now it suddenly opened without anyone knocking. The hotel manager walked in, clutching a screwdriver.

Wang Bin knew the man was in charge of the hotel. He had seen him through a door behind the reception desk when he had checked in, but had not spoken to him.

The girl at the reception desk had noticed Wang Bin's Beijing accent and immediately suggested one of the more expensive rooms. She was young, fresh-looking, probably told to recommend expensive rooms to anyone who was not a regular. She had a pleasant, welcoming smile and spoke with a heavily slurred local accent, which he found quite charming if not always easy to follow.

He had heard it at close quarters on the bus to Pingyang. The man sitting next to him had offered a cigarette and then, when he realized Wang Bin was from Beijing, had proceeded to entertain him with stories about one of the local farmers. The farmer in question had gone to Beijing and made good. He would come back to his hometown every Spring Festival to see his relatives and of course pay his respects to Chief Han. There was no envy or disapproval in the man's voice when he told the story. There was rather pride that he knew of someone who had gone off to the big city and done well.

Wang Bin had wanted to ask who Chief Han was, but it was not easy to stop the man's flow once he had got going, and by the time there was a pause, the subject of his monologue had changed.

Somewhat annoyed that the hotel manager had burst into his room without warning, Wang Bin sat up from where he was lying on his bed. He did not let on that he knew who the intruder was. Instead he spoke angrily.

'What the hell do you think you're doing barging in like this. Don't they give you any training in this hotel?'

The manager narrowed his eyes and walked across to the air-conditioner.

'Just come to check the cooler's working okay.'

He moved Wang Bin's knapsack from the chair to the floor next to the desk.

'Hey! Be careful with that bag. There's photographic equipment in there.'

The manager did not offer an apology. He simply pulled the now-empty chair into the corner beneath the air-conditioner, climbed onto it and started fiddling with the switches and vents on the panel.

Wang Bin watched him, looked at the man's dirty shoes digging into the worn fabric of the chair. He was poking the air-conditioner with his screwdriver.

'How long are you staying then?'

Wang Bin had left that part of the guest registration form blank. The hotel manager must have inspected it.

'I'm not sure. A few days, maybe a week.'

The man turned, looked down at him.

'Most people just pass through. One night. Two at the most.'

He waited for Wang Bin's reaction to this, looking him over, summing him up, wondering what advantage he could get out of this stranger from the far-off capital.

'Do they?' Wang Bin said, not offering any more information.

The manager changed his tack, got onto the subject he had really come into the room for.

'You want me to arrange a girl for you tonight then?'

It was Wang Bin's turn to narrow his eyes.

'You know you can be arrested for making a proposition like that. What are you, some kind of pimp? There's nothing wrong with the air-conditioner. Clear off and let me get some rest.'

The manager gave Wang Bin a long, cold look, climbed down from the chair, made no attempt to put it back next to the table, and retreated without closing the door behind him.

His journey from Beijing had taken him first to Xian then Chengdu and Chongqing and finally the long dusty ride to Pingyang. In each of the modest hotels he had stayed in, he had found the phone in his room ringing late in the evening, girls offering to give him a massage or whatever else tickled his fancy. He had hoped to get away from the sleazier side of travel once he had left the big cities and got to this small country town, which he had planned to use as his base. But now, he was angry and indignant that the hotel manager seemed to think it quite normal to run the place like a brothel, flouting the teachings of Mao and the directives of the central government. Wang Bin was a good party member and disapproved of the way the law was ignored more and more blatantly the farther the perpetrator found himself from Beijing.

Wang Bin was no longer in the mood for sleep. He got up and took out the copy of *International Birdwatcher's Digest* with Ben Hadlock's drawing of the Mountain Phoenix and once more studied it reverently. Then, making sure his other bag was locked, he took his knapsack containing his expensive camera equipment and made his way to the hotel reception and entrance, intending to go for an exploratory stroll around town.

The same girl was manning the reception desk. There was a hint of approval, almost of admiration, in the way she smiled at him. It occurred to Wang Bin that she was aware of the outcome of the manager's visit to his room. Perhaps she disapproved as much as he did about the goings on in the hotel. She certainly looked too young and innocent to be a player in the game.

He walked up to the counter and deposited his key.

'Is your room okay?'

She spoke pleasantly as if wanting to engage Wang Bin in a longer dialogue. Perhaps he seemed different to her, different from the usual clientele, not just because of his accent.

'Yes, but I want you to register a complaint with your manager about the workman who came in to fix the air-conditioner.'

He paused, glancing at the door behind the reception desk. It was ajar.

'That workman should be given the sack. Dragging

down the name of your hotel.'

The girl was beginning to look uncomfortable. Wang Bin sensed that she knew the manager was in the room behind the reception desk; could hear every word he was saying. She did not make any attempt to encourage him to elaborate his complaint, made no conciliatory murmur of any kind. She just looked at him wide-eyed, wishing today had been her day off.

Wang Bin's sense of outrage was gathering momentum. He disregarded the girl's discomfort.

'He offered to sell me a prostitute for the night. I've a good mind to report him to the local Party Secretariat. You don't want people thinking this hotel is some kind of brothel. It won't do. It really won't do. Tell your manager to get rid of him. He's a liability. No self-respecting person will want to stay here if that sort of rumour gets around …'

He had finished. The poor girl looked terribly embarrassed.

'I'll report your complaint to him.'

Wang Bin smiled more kindly at her.

Then reading her name on the badge she was wearing pinned to her uniform, 'Thank you, Miss Zhou Jun. May I call you Xiao Zhou?' He was trying to appear more friendly and informal, after all his complaint had nothing to do with the girl herself.

'Now then. Which is the way to the river?'

Xiao Zhou was relieved to be talking about something different.

'Take any of the side streets across the road. If you want to go to Martyrs Bridge it's to the right after you reach the riverbank. You can't miss it. A series of arches. It's all lit up in the evening. And there are lots of places to eat.'

He thanked her and made his way out into the bright sunshine. He crossed to the other side of the main street.

When he had gone, Manager Wu came out of his office.

'Stuck-up Beijinger. Thinks he knows everything. He could do with being taught a lesson, the little prick.'

The girl lowered her eyes. She knew it was best not to say anything when Manager Wu was in one of his disgruntled moods.

Just at that moment, Han San Xi, the town's Chief of Police, came through the front entrance of the hotel.

2

Han San Xi was a short, round man with small black eyes and a nose that curved at the end like an eagle's beak. He had thick, black hair, which he kept swept off his shining, fat forehead in a blow wave, thanks to frequent visits to the local barber's shop. The girls there always made a fuss of him. He liked to joke and flaunt his wealth as he handed out tips with one hand while running the other over the recipient's buttocks. The girls did not mind. He was generous and they knew that by staying in his good books they could safely make other money on the side. Sometimes he would provide them with evening work, if he had a guest in town or if he wanted to show a gesture of thanks to one of his helpers at the conclusion of a lucrative business transaction.

Had Han San Xi been a good man he would doubtless have done great things for Pingyang. The path he had chosen, however, was one of corruption and self-enrichment. He had become powerful by being greedy and kindling greed in others. The whole town knew him and he knew everything that was going on in the town. He knew who the regular truck drivers were, the travelling salesmen, the itinerant workers. There were plenty of people who wanted to ingratiate themselves with him. His network of informants permeated every house, shop and business establishment and provided him with the information he needed to remain powerful and increase his wealth.

His staff on the police force ensured that any opposition to his will was quickly reversed or eliminated.

He had an intuitive understanding of human weakness and used this to his advantage, handing out small doses of what each person wanted, ensuring that they soon craved for more. He manipulated people until they became addicted to him. The fabric of his influence was so pervading, so finely woven, that he was able to merge in people's minds the concept of integrity with that of loyalty to his person.

It was not surprising therefore that the arrival of any stranger by bus was soon brought to his attention.

In the hotel, Manager Wu greeted Chief Han with enthusiasm and led him through to his office, closing the door behind them.

'Delighted to see you as always. Tea? Or something stronger?'

'Tea'll do.'

Manager Wu went to the cupboard where he kept the tin of first grade *longjin cha* reserved for Chief Han's visits. He shook some tea leaves into the bottom of a clean glass and then half filled the glass with boiling water from a thermos flask. He put the flask back on the floor next to the low coffee table where Chief Han was sitting and sat down himself in the chair opposite.

'Busy?' Chief Han said as he pulled a cigarette from a flat silver cigarette case engraved with a dragon snorting flames between outstretched claws. He did not offer one to Manager Wu.

'So-so. We'll have our regular crowd in on Saturday.'

Saturday was the day most guests stayed over at the hotel, breaking their journey to and from Chongqing.

'I hear there's a foreigner in town.'

For Chief Han, anyone outside a radius of a hundred kilometres was a foreigner.

'Yeah. Some stuck-up young know-it-all from Beijing. Got all agitated when I offered to find him something to cuddle at night. Said he'd report me to the local party secretariat if you please. Wouldn't say how long he's staying. He's just stepped out. Surprised you didn't see him on your way in.'

'Party member is he? Why d'you think he's in Pingyang?'

'No idea. He's got a whole load of camera equipment though. Obviously wants to take pictures of something.'

'Well if he sets foot in Dongjin Street I'll make sure Comrade Zhang gives him the bum's rush.'

He took a sleek, shiny, gold-coloured mobile phone from its leather sheath attached to his belt like a gun holster, and dialled a number.

'Comrade Zhang? ... Yeah, it's me ... No, I'm at the Merchants Hotel with Lao Wu ... I've heard you may get a visitor sometime today complaining about him. Some youngster just got in. All the way from Beijing. Give him a hard time. See you later tonight at Da Jie Jie's.'

He clicked the off button with his thumbnail, folded the mobile phone shut and tucked it back in its sheath.

'That should sort him out if he tries anything funny. I'll tell my men, too, to show him he's not welcome if they see him around town. Don't be surprised if he checks out tomorrow.'

Both men laughed.

The tea in Chief Han's glass had had time to infuse. The tea leaves had unfurled and settled at the bottom. Manager Wu picked up the flask again and filled the glass. He then topped up his own, an old coffee jar with a screw cap, which he kept in his office at the hotel and carried with him everywhere, whenever he went out. Chief Han lifted his glass and took a sniff at the tea without drinking any.

'Which room have you put him in?'

'One-oh-four.'

'Ground floor opposite the kitchens?'

'That's it.'

'Good choice. Let's go and look through his stuff.'

The two men made their way out of the office and across the courtyard to Wang Bin's room, which Manager Wu opened with a master key attached to his belt. They checked the lock on the black leather bag and, unable to open it without force, felt the contents from the outside.

'Seems to be only clothes in here. He was carrying his camera bag with him when he went out just now.'

Chief Han picked up the *International Birdwatcher's Digest* magazine lying open on the table. He could not read English and knew Manager Wu did not know any either. They both looked at the drawing of the Mountain Phoenix, then turned the page and saw other detailed sketches Hadlock had made of other wildlife in the area.

'He's probably another of those birdwatchers here on holiday with his camera. Nothing to worry about. Doesn't mean we can't have some fun with him though.'

He turned to leave the room, Manager Wu in his wake, and went back to the main building.

'No, I won't stay longer. Let me know though when our friend gets back.'

'Where will you be?'

Manager Wu knew full well that Chief Han was planning to go to Da Jie Jie's that evening. He had of course been to Da Jie Jie's many a time but had never been invited to join one of the Chief's parties. Perhaps now the Chief might think of asking him to come along. His connection with the Chief would be put on a different footing, people would respect him more, if he was seen invited just once to join the Chief's inner circle of cronies.

Chief Han only told Manager Wu to call him on his mobile phone.

He was soon driving back to the police headquarters by Martyrs Bridge .

Driving himself was much more satisfying than being

driven. The Mitsubishi Jeep was the only one of its kind in town. It was big and powerful, appropriately so for his position. When he sat behind the wheel, he was higher off the road, looking down on the other cars and drivers. He had ordered the vehicle to be delivered with all available optional gadgets: extra fog lamps fixed to the bumper; huge searchlights on the roof that could beam out in all directions; an external loudspeaker system that made dogs, chickens and children scamper out of his way, and old grandmothers pause in their sleep. When he was in his jeep it felt like he was in the turret of his private tank. He had asked for an automatic weapon to be fixed on the roof between the searchlights, but the manufacturers had said that it was not on their list of optional accessories, even if he had seen one in an American action movie.

Back in his office he gave a directive to his men to keep an eye out for the new arrival from Beijing, and find some excuse to make him feel uncomfortable. He then retired to his couch to be fresh for his evening visit to Da Jie Jie's.

Xiao Zhou had heard Manager Wu and Chief Han talking about the young visitor from Beijing and felt sorry for him.

She had seen how vindictive both men could be when they wanted to. When she had first got her job at the hotel, she had been very enthusiastic. Her parents had had to pay some money under the table in order for her to get it and she wanted to prove her worth as much to them as to the hotel management. Then, when she had been asked to do night duty, she had hesitated, but accepted. However, when Manager Wu suggested she serve drinks in the rooms where the guests gathered on Saturday nights to play mahjong she flatly refused.

'Yu Mei can go. I'll stay on duty at the reception desk.'

Yu Mei was one of the other night-duty girls, and Xiao Zhou did not like her at all. She thought she overdid her make-up and was not surprised that she had to push guests' wandering hands away, albeit not too abruptly. But Yu Mei did not have Xiao Zhou's looks, and Manager Wu would have dearly liked Xiao Zhou to be friendlier with the guests.

Because of her resistance, Manager Wu took a dislike to her and would have given her notice had Chief Han not interceded and told him to put her on day duty again.

'We'll find other girls for the night shifts. Use Xiao Zhou during the day to lend the hotel a bit of respectability. She's sure anyway to come round in the end when she sees how much the others are making.'

But Xiao Zhou did not 'come round' and stayed on permanently doing the day shifts and not caring in the least that her monthly salary was only a fraction of what Yu Mei and the others got.

She got ready for Yu Mei to come in at six to take over her duty at the reception desk.

Tomorrow was her day off and this evening she was planning to eat out at the restaurants by Martyrs Bridge. Perhaps she would meet some of her old classmates there. Perhaps come across the young man from Beijing. She might even have a chance to tip him off about Manager Wu and Chief Han taking an interest in him.

When Yu Mei arrived, Xiao Zhou was almost relieved that Wang Bin had not yet returned to the hotel. She was bound now to bump into him in town. She would keep her eyes open.

'Any business tonight?' Yu Mei asked Manager Wu, ignoring Xiao Zhou as she slipped out of her coat and put on her uniform jacket, leaving the top button casually undone as she always did.

'No, very quiet. There's one guest from out of town but he won't be staying long. There might be some rooms taken later on after Da Jie Jie's. Chief Han's got a party on over there. But I expect she'll be able accommodate all the guests who want to stay over.'

Manager Wu was not very pleased that his establishment was only used to take the overflow.

Saturday was different though. Saturday always saw his regular clientele arrive. Sometimes he was understaffed, but a call to Chief Han always sorted that sort of problem out.

Xiao Zhou put on her light coat, pulled the belt tight around her waist, wished them both a pleasant evening and set off in the direction of Martyrs Bridge.

'Little Miss Innocence that one,' said Yu Mei as soon as Xiao Zhou was gone. 'Acting as if she's never been screwed.'

'I wouldn't be surprised if she never has been,' said Manager Wu.

'Oh really? I thought it was part of your interview procedure.'

3

Wang Bin found his way to the river easily enough and just as Xiao Zhou had said, saw Martyrs Bridge about a kilometre upstream to his right.

It was after five and the early evening sunlight caught the warm-coloured stonework of the bridge's arches. They cast a reflection in the puddles of still water left in patches over the stony riverbed. It was late summer and the river at this time of year was reduced to a trickle. Wang Bin noticed the stains on the stone walls shoring up the riverbank where he was standing and realized that the water level must rise dramatically in spring after the melting of the mountain snows.

He looked once more towards Martyrs Bridge. There were seven arches in all, oddly unsymmetrical. From the town side, five arches rose gradually as the bridge stretched out across the river, each one slightly taller than the previous. Then the last two arches were smaller again as the bridge reached the opposite bank, not with a sudden drop, but with a soft falling away like a wave that had spent its energy. This made the bridge look lop-sided, particularly as the summer trickle of water chose to flow under the middle arch and not the tallest. He wondered if the river had at some time in the past slightly changed its course and the town decided to add more arches to compensate. But he could not see any evidence of new stonework. Each slab looked equally old and weather-beaten.

On the side of the river where he was standing, houses with crooked wooden walls and sagging roof tiles stretched in the direction of Martyrs Bridge. The houses were perched unevenly on the riverbank like bedraggled cormorants. There was no path to walk along between the houses and the river.

The opposite bank of the river had no houses at all, only a patchwork of fields and vegetable plots stretching to the base of the hills. These rose, steep and dark mauve-coloured, contrasting with the snow-capped mountains behind.

At the end of the side road he had taken to reach the river, some stone steps descended to the riverbed. To reach Martyrs Bridge he could either take these steps and then clamber across the stones and sandy patches of the riverbed, or retrace his steps and try to find an alley running behind the houses on the riverbank.

A group of women was washing clothes in the stream some way off in the centre of the riverbed. The water could not be that muddy. He decided to use this route to reach the bridge. One of the women looked up as he passed by. He was too far from them to say anything. He waved a greeting. She just nodded as she continued scrubbing the clothes. She must have said something to the other two. They turned their heads towards Wang Bin, pausing in their work.

When he reached the bridge he found some more steps leading up out of the river. He climbed these and emerged into a street that was a flurry of activity.

This was the focal point of the town and there were rows of restaurants on each side of the street, as far as the crossroads. Strung between the trees outside the restaurants were electric light bulbs inviting guests to inspect the food, which the restaurant owners had put on display, ready to serve up in any way desired.

Wang Bin was not hungry yet, but enjoyed the carnival-like atmosphere and was happy to stroll along, smiling and joking with the restaurant owners as they endeavoured to entice him into their four-tabled eating rooms.

'It's too early to eat.'

'Ah but you will be able to choose the choicest morsels.'

A speciality of Pingyang appeared to be the live animals outside each restaurant waiting to be selected for the chopping block and wok. There were pigeons, rabbits and rodents, each species in a separate cage. Their eyes gleamed timidly under the string of electric bulbs.

Next to them, inside makeshift containers made of chicken wire, lay pans of slimy toads clambering over each other or just sitting, unblinking, watching the passers-by. A bright red plastic bowl was full of dark green eels slithering left and right into a slippery tangle of living strands of flesh, waiting to be gutted.

A few guests were already eating, others were dawdling outside the restaurants inspecting the menus on offer in the cages, deciding which establishment to patronize.

Wang Bin was beginning to build up an appetite as he wandered along the stretch of road unaware that he was being observed by two policemen sitting in their vehicle parked on the other side.

Suddenly he stopped dead in his tracks. He stood staring into an old bamboo cage outside one of the restaurants.

There, unmistakably, standing forlornly at the bottom, amidst scattered droppings and some dried up slithers of fish, silvery and shiny like the droppings, was a Mountain Phoenix.

He squatted beside the cage to inspect the bird more closely. It did not shy away from him into a corner, but just stood where it was, stoically accepting its captivity. Wang Bin imagined it had resigned itself to its fate, had given up trying to struggle free.

The bird was a beautiful specimen.

Orange eyes stared back at him, black outlines around them shining as if freshly painted. The plumage on the head was dark brown between the eyes, turning to fawn and ending in a bright pillar-box red on top with two scarlet plumes sweeping back like the trailing eyebrows of a learned hermit. The beak was straight and pointed, bright orange, like the eyes, with two nose holes amidst tiny white feathers where it was attached to the head. The bird's breast was golden orange, finely outlined in black, its wings were greyish with shimmering shades of blue and metallic green and its tail long and slender with two feathers fanning out at the end resembling sparkling emeralds. Its legs were pale yellow, thin and lanky, the legs of a wading bird, but the feet were not webbed. They had strong claws accustomed to grasping and holding on.

Wang Bin was in a state of shock. He had come to Pingyang to scour the mountain forests in the hope of catching a glimpse of a Mountain Phoenix. The last thing he had expected was to find one in a cage outside a restaurant. He was both delighted to see it at close quarters and enraged that it should be in captivity, waiting to be killed.

The restaurant owner came up behind him.

'You can have it grilled with wild mushrooms or deep fried with chilli and garlic.'

Wang Bin just stared up at him.

'It can be ready in twenty minutes. Try some sliced air-dried wild boar with some cold beer while you're waiting.' The man tried to hand Wang Bin a dirty menu covered in a creased, clear plastic sheet. Then, taking his silence for hesitation, he continued: 'You won't find a beauty like this anywhere else here. Some farmers brought it in this morning. Caught it in the mountains. Paid them a handsome price for it. Reckon it was worth it.'

His eyes, sharp as a sniper's, wandered to Wang Bin's bulging waist pouch.

'Give me a round thousand and I'll do a special dish for

you any way you want it cooked. You should try it with the wild mushrooms, though. You won't be disappointed.'

Wang Bin was shocked at the price the man was asking for the bird. Even in the best restaurants in Beijing you would not pay that much for a dish. He reckoned it would be useless to tell the man the bird was an endangered species. He fully intended to set it free again. After, of course, taking some photos of the exquisite specimen. But he did not want to seem too keen and cause the price to start escalating before he could conclude his transaction.

'A thousand yuan is far too much for a bird as small as this. There's hardly any meat on it.'

'You're not from round here then?'

The restaurant owner focused on Wang Bin's accent rather than his bargaining banter.

'No, I'm just visiting.'

'All the more reason for you to try something different. You won't get a chance to eat anything like this where you come from.'

The man, deft as an accomplished magician, produced a long, shining, sharp knife from a pocket in his apron.

'What do you say, then?'

Wang Bin was aghast.

'No. Stop. I don't want to eat it. It's far too beautiful. I want to keep it.'

The restaurant owner could see he was going to conclude his sale.

'Why not. It only eats fish though. Tiddly ones. I've got a few I can let you have until you get a supply of your own. Don't expect to teach it to sing, now. It can only do a high-pitched whistle.'

As if on cue, the bird emitted a screech from the cage.

Wang Bin was ecstatic. He was actually listening to the song of a live Mountain Phoenix. He could not believe his luck.

'A thousand yuan then, with the fish and the cage.'

'Can't let you have the cage. I'll still need it. I can let you have a hemp sack and a plastic tray. You can put the tray inside and tie the sack tight at the top. Plenty of room in there for the bird to breathe until you sort out a proper cage.'

Wang Bin unzipped his waist pouch and pulled ten hundred-yuan bills from it. The man took the notes and held them up to the light with both hands, rubbing each one as if he was washing a dirty handkerchief. 'There're a lot of fake ones around these days,' he said. He pocketed the money and added: 'You'd better watch out, walking around with a great wad of money like that.'

Wang Bin's hand went defensively to the pouch at his waist. His fingers touched the zip as if to check that he had not left it open.

The man went inside and then through to the yard at the back of the restaurant. He took a hemp sack from a pile in the corner next to another cage with a pigeon in it waiting to be put on display outside the restaurant later in the evening. The sack had string threaded around the top so that it could be pulled tight.

He came back with the sack and tossed it on top of the cage containing the Mountain Phoenix.

'Might as well eat first. How about something else if you don't want me to cook the bird? There's a lovely pair of bull toads in that bucket.'

Wang Bin was tempted but thought he should get the bird back to his hotel room as quickly as possible, take some photos of it, and find out how to get up into the mountains early next morning to set it free.

So he helped the restaurant owner prepare the plastic tray and put it together with an open container of small fish at the bottom of the sack. Then Wang Bin carefully removed the bird from its cage. As he held it firmly but gently in his hands he was surprised that it did not struggle. He felt the warmth of its body against his palms, the softness of its breast feathers against his fingers. He raised it to eye level and looked long and lovingly at the bird's head with its gorgeous plumage. He was so glad he had made the arduous journey to Pingyang. His reward was beyond his wildest dreams.

Clutching the sack and taking care not to swing it about too much as he walked, he started making his way back to the Pingyang Merchants Hotel, this time using the main street rather than the riverbed route.

He had not gone a hundred metres past the crossroads when a police car pulled up alongside him and the two officers who had been watching him earlier got out. One of them raised his right hand to his cap in the customary salute the police used before handing out a fine. The traffic police were notorious for their sadistic politeness. A two finger salute to their caps, two hundred yuan in Chief Han's pocket and a percentage of this in theirs.

'Good evening,' said Wang Bin cautiously.

'Identity card' – a pause to eye their prey at close quarters – 'if you please.'

4

Xiao Zhou saw Wang Bin being pushed into the back of the police car with his knapsack and another bag. He seemed to be more concerned about the other bag than himself, carrying it carefully, protecting it with both arms as the policemen shoved him from behind. Some passers-by stopped to watch. Xiao Zhou quickened her pace and reached the car just as the driver closed his door. Wang Bin looked out of the window and recognized Xiao Zhou. He leant forward in his seat as if about to say something but was pushed back by the policeman sitting next to him. There was a worried, pleading look in his eyes as they met Xiao Zhou's.

'What's the matter?' she said to the driver as he started the engine.

The policeman looked up at her.

'What's he done?' she persisted.

The driver put the car in gear and held it with the clutch.

'D'you know this man?' he asked.

'Not exactly. He's just checked into our hotel.'

'Mind yer own business then.'

He revved the engine and started swivelling the steering wheel to do a U-turn in the road.

She ran next to the driver's open window.

'Where are you taking him?'

'To see Chief Han.'

The car finished the U-turn and headed back towards Martyrs Bridge and the police headquarters.

Xiao Zhou stood in the middle of the road wondering what to do. She felt an impulse to help the young man. Two years before an old fellow had fallen off his bicycle. The crate of empty bottles he had been balancing precariously behind him had crashed to the ground and the man had cut himself quite badly on the broken glass. She had instinctively gone to his aid. Without thinking twice. Had helped him up. Getting blood all over her dress in the process. This, now, too was a 'don't-think-twice' situation and she strode off towards the police headquarters and Chief Han's office.

The police car pulled into the courtyard of the police headquarters and Wang Bin was escorted up some steps to the main hall. The policeman who had been sitting in the back of the car with Wang Bin spoke to the officer on duty.

'Found him loitering suspiciously. Thought you'd like to question him.'

At first Wang Bin was indignant.

'What the hell's all this about? Is there some law against walking along the street?'

Just as he had done when the policemen first stopped him at the roadside, he pulled out his identity card as well as his party membership card from his waist pouch, exposing the wad of notes he had tucked away there.

The officer looked at Wang Bin, not at the cards he had placed on the counter.

Wang Bin continued in a less aggressive tone.

'There seems to have been some mistake. I'm sure it can all be cleared up.'

But the officer on duty did not smile. He took the two cards from the counter top, relieved Wang Bin of his knapsack as well as the other bag he was carrying, but did not take the waist pouch from him. He then directed another officer to take Wang Bin to an interview room along a corridor at the back of the station.

'You two can get back on duty,' he said to the two

policemen who had brought Wang Bin in.

The second officer told Wang Bin to sit at a table in the interview room and made to leave. Wang Bin stopped him.

'Look here,' he said again but this time much more nervously, his mouth was beginning to go dry. 'Is there a senior officer I can speak to? Or someone from Pingyang's Party Secretariat?'

The officer left the room without answering. Wang Bin's palms began to sweat.

What seemed like a very long ten minutes later, the first officer who had taken Wang Bin's belongings came into the room carrying his bags and placed them on the table.

'And what have we here then?' he said coldly.

The knapsack straps had been loosened, the flaps were still open. They had gone through its contents.

'If you've damaged my camera …' Indignation crept back into Wang Bin's tone of voice despite himself.

'And this?' The officer pointed at the hemp sack containing the bird Wang Bin had just bought. They had inspected its contents too.

'It's a bird. I've just bought it. I'm an enthusiast. Look, can't I speak with your senior officer and clear up this misunderstanding.'

'You think I'm not senior enough do you? Think I can't sort you out?'

'No, I didn't mean that. I just want to explain.'

'I'm listening.' He pulled out a notebook and pencil from his breast pocket and leant back in his chair, glaring at Wang Bin.

'It's a Mountain Phoenix, on the endangered species list. The chap who sold it to me didn't know. I was trying to save it. Set it free.'

'Is that so now? Doesn't look that free to me. Tied up in a sack.'

'It's only temporary. I didn't have a cage. The man wouldn't let me buy the cage he had it in.'

The officer scribbled in his notebook as Wang Bin told his story. When he had finished speaking, the officer stood up.

'You wait here, and don't tamper with the evidence while I'm gone.'

'Of course not. Anything you say.'

He was tempted to check that his camera was all right while the officer was out of the room, but the thought of his coming back in and catching him red-handed kept his hands away from the knapsack.

But the officer did not come back for another half an hour and by then Wang Bin was growing more frantic by the minute.

When he finally returned, he was still unsmiling.

'Come with me. Bring those bags with you.'

He led his prisoner down a corridor to a much more elaborately ornate door at the end with a polished brass handle. He knocked, opened the door and ushered Wang Bin inside.

Chief Han looked up from behind his desk.

'Leave us.'

The officer left Wang Bin standing in the room and retreated, closing the door quietly behind him.

Half an hour earlier, Xiao Zhou had been standing in exactly the same spot. She had managed to persuade the officer on duty at the front counter to tell Chief Han she was in the building and wanted to see him.

The officer had been reluctant at first. He had already interrupted the Chief to tell him they had picked up the Beijinger and put him in the interview room, that he was carrying a wad of notes on him, had expensive-looking camera equipment and a bird in a bag.

'A what?'

'A bird, sir. Says it's an endangered species. That he's just bought it and was planning to set it free.'

'Is that so now? He's making it easier and easier for us now, isn't he?'

So when Xiao Zhou said she wanted to see Chief Han, the officer told her it was out of the question.

'Chief Han's a busy man. You can't just turn up and expect him to see you. What's the problem? I'll handle it.'

She had had to think quickly. If she said she had come about Wang Bin she was sure to be shown the door. Then she remembered Manager Wu talking about Chief Han's party tonight at Da Jie Jie's.

'It's about the party at Da Jie Jie's tonight.'

The officer raised his eyebrows. He was used to categorizing people and Xiao Zhou definitely did not fit into the Da Jie Jie box. But she did know about Chief Han's plans and it might be a mistake on his part not to tell the Chief she was here. So he told her to wait while he checked if the Chief wanted to see her.

'Who?' Chief Han said, irritated at being interrupted a second time.

'Xiao Zhou. From the Merchants Hotel.'

'What's she want?'

'Wouldn't say much. Something about a party at Da Jie Jie's. Shall I tell her you're busy?'

Chief Han thought for a moment. Lao Wu must have sent her with a message, though why he had not called him on his mobile phone he did not know.

'Show her in. And let that prick from Beijing sweat it out by himself until I'm ready to see him.'

By the time Xiao Zhou had been lead down the long corridor to Chief Han's office, her confidence was beginning to ebb. Then standing in the big office, she began to tremble. But Chief Han stood up and came over to her. He took her by the arm and sat her down on the settee while he, himself, took the armchair next to it.

'So, what's Manager Wu want to tell me that he can't tell me over the phone?'

She looked at him, puzzled.

'It's nothing to do with Manager Wu. I've come about Mr Wang.'

Chief Han's blank expression encouraged her to clarify who she was talking about.

'Wang Bin, the young man from Beijing who checked into

the hotel this afternoon. I heard you talking to Manager Wu about him and now he's just been picked up in the street by your policemen and brought here. What's he done wrong?'

The Chief's cordiality disappeared.

'What's that got to do with you?'

Xiao Zhou wished now she had not come to the police headquarters. What was it to her if the Beijinger had got himself into trouble. He might even really be a crook for all she knew.

'Nothing. I don't even know him. It's just that I saw him a short while ago being put into a police car. He saw me, too, and seemed to want me to help. I don't suppose he knows anyone here. Should I tell Manager Wu what's happened. What if someone phones from Beijing for him. I mean. Is it serious what he's done? He seemed all right to me. Respectable sort of chap. Isn't he?'

Behind a stern face, Chief Han hid his amusement at the girl's fumbling nervousness.

'We will deal with him appropriately.'

Then more kindly as he leant forward in his chair closer to Xiao Zhou.

'Don't worry your pretty little head over him. He's upset Manager Wu and we're going to persuade him to leave town tomorrow, so you won't have any phone calls from Beijing to deal with. Just tell anyone who calls he's checked out and moved on.'

Xiao Zhou sat there thinking she had already taken up far too much of Chief Han's time and that she should go but he did not make any gesture to indicate that he wanted her to. He just sat there looking closely at her. She began to feel uncomfortable again and thought she should say something to break the silence that had settled on their meeting.

'He was carrying a bag, some sort of sack, when he was picked up. He didn't have it when he left the hotel. If that information's any use to you.'

'He bought a bird. Says it's an endangered species. Wants to set it free if you please.'

'A bird? Really? What a lovely idea.'

Her face was shining now. She knew she had been right about the young man all along. He really was a decent fellow.

'Can I see him?'

'No, you can't. I haven't questioned him yet. He'll be sent back to the hotel later tonight. But then, of course, you won't be on duty, will you?'

Chief Han's thoughts wandered to Da Jie Jie's party.

'Why not come along to Da Jie Jie's? I've got a small get-together there with a group of friends tonight. I see you already seem to know about it. How about it then?'

'No thank you. I have to go now.'

She stood up waiting for Chief Han to show her out, which he did, guiding her to the door with his arm across her shoulders.

'You know, I could be real good to you, Xiao Zhou. You just need to loosen up a bit. Think about it.'

He opened the door and saw her out.

Sitting back at his desk, he cracked his knuckles, picked up the phone and said: 'Send the lad in now.'

5

Wang Bin stood in the middle of the room clutching his bags, looking at Chief Han who was leaning back in an enormous black leather chair behind his desk. His office always had an awesome effect on anyone entering it for the first time and Chief Han liked to savour the moment when each new visitor stood there taking it all in, his power, his position.

Wang Bin had never been in a government office with fittings of such extravagance. The carpet was deep red. He felt its thick pile under his shoes. The walls were panelled in beech and had extraordinarily gaudy light fittings sticking out at intervals. Lampshades made of pieces of coloured glass were fixed on top of intertwined brass supports, sprouting bunches of grapes dangling between curling vine leaves. Chief Han had had the vine leaves painted green and the grapes blue.

From the centre of the ceiling hung an enormous glass chandelier.

The room itself was huge.

On one side there was a window looking out over the river and under this a settee with two armchairs in maroon-coloured leather. The arms were solid wood finished in a glossy varnish and carved in the shape of a swan's neck, head and beak, turned towards the carpet as if preparing to vomit. At the bottom were carved, webbed feet, each thick and heavy on top of a square wooden block, as if the birds were standing on a Beijing opera actor's high wooden shoe, about to perform some acrobatic feat.

In front of the settee was a tiger skin rug and on top of that, a low glass coffee table. The coffee table had no legs. It rested on the ears and upturned trunk of a brass elephant's head.

Chief Han's desk occupied most of the other side of the room. Like the room, it was oversized. Its glossily varnished wooden top, the shape of a pentagon sliced in two, jutting out into the room like a sickle in mid-swing.

On the desk, at one end, there was a solitary black phone. At the other, stood a painted wooden carving, almost a metre tall, of an eagle, wings and talons outstretched and beak open ready to attack. Its would-be prey was a similarly poised cobra, rising from its coils, hood open, fixing the eagle with its stare.

In the centre of the desk, on the side a guest might sit if invited to, was a large bronze toad, the size of four men's fists, sitting on top of a pile of coins welded haphazardly together, the old sort with square holes through the middle. The body of the toad was encrusted with fake rubies, its eyes were two tiny round glass emeralds and in its mouth it held yet another bronze coin.

There was enough room to walk all around the desk and Chief Han often did so while thinking through a problem. He always worked out his plans of action in his head and never wrote anything down. His ability to do this and to compartmentalize each thought was one of the reasons for his success in life. It also enabled him to keep his desktop clear of any paper, so that the gloss of the varnish could be seen and his two treasured ornaments appear even more prominent. Only the black phone reminded the visitor that the piece of furniture was a desk.

Wang Bin stood, taking in his surroundings. Chief Han sat, studying his prey.

Wang Bin thought it better to wait to be asked to speak

or sit. Chief Han finally gestured to his guest to take the chair opposite him, next to the bronze toad. He put his bags on the floor beside the chair and sat down.

'Officer Liao has spoken to me about you.'

Wang Bin remained sitting stiffly upright on the chair.

'Look, are you in charge here?'

Chief Han's eyes flashed angrily.

Wang Bin continued.

'Of course you must be. Well, sir, there's been some silly mistake. Your men ...'

'There's been no mistake, Mr Wang. My 'men' as you call them have done a commendable job. Caught you red-handed I believe. Smuggling an endangered species.'

It never occurred to Wang Bin that he might be taken for a smuggler. Chief Han's unexpected accusation now caught him off guard.

'I wasn't intending to keep the bird.'

'That's not what you told Li Hai Shan.' Then, seeing Wang Bin's puzzled look, the Chief added: 'The restaurant owner.'

Wang Bin became defensive.

'He was going to cook the poor thing. If that's not criminal I ...'

Chief Han's fist came thumping down on his desk making the toad hop, the chandelier tinkle and Wang Bin freeze in his seat.

'You're the person being investigated here. Trading in endangered species is a serious crime.'

He stood up and started pacing around the desk.

'And smuggling them out of my jurisdiction under my very nose doesn't warm me to you.'

He was now next to the chair where Wang Bin was sitting, bearing down on him with his small black eyes and beak-like nose. Wang Bin remained frozen, waiting for the next swooping attack. He realized he ought not to have told the restaurant owner he was going to keep the bird. The man must have reported him, but as to the reason why, he had no idea.

'We've had directives from Central Government to stamp out this kind of activity.'

The Chief had resumed his pacing.

'The mountains around Pingyang are teaming with rare specimens. We try to work closely with the local police force on the other side of the border over these matters, but still too many smugglers slip through our nets and our motherland's wildlife ends up stuffed in a glass box, in some

American's collection, while the unpatriotic traitor who sold it enjoys a fat profit.'

He paused, thinking he was doing really well this time. The wimp on the chair was beginning to turn positively paler.

'Last year we rounded up a group of farmers who had killed a tiger.'

His eyes wandered beyond his prey to the tiger skin rug at the other end of the room.

'We got there too late. They had already pulled the animals teeth, sliced off its penis and balls and smuggled the stuff out to Shanghai.'

There was a note of outrage in his voice.

'The ringleader paid dearly for his treachery.' Chief Han pulled his forefinger from left to right across his neck.

The ringleader of course had not been executed, merely fined, and Chief Han's outrage was about the man's treachery towards the Chief himself, by carrying out some illegal activity without giving him his cut, even though he had ended up with a tiger skin rug for his office.

'I'm not a smuggler. Really I'm not.'

Wang Bin's plea was barely audible.

'Who are your accomplices now?'

The Chief was back on the offensive, once more relishing the situation.

'I don't know anyone here. Really I don't. I'm just an ornithologist trying to get some photos of wildlife.'

'To show to your customers in Shanghai, no doubt?'

'No.' It came out as a shout. Wang Bin was really frightened now.

'You can't accuse me unjustly like this. I'm not that sort of person. I have my Ornithological Society membership card right here.'

He fumbled in his waist pouch and held the card up to the Chief, looking him straight in the eyes, defiantly.

Chief Han began to smile slowly.

'Don't you go raising your voice with me, you lump of dog's shit. You're in deep trouble and right now I'm the only one who can help you. If I choose to. I still haven't decided whether or not to call Officer Liao in and have him put you in the lock-up until you can be formally charged in court. And you know what *that* means.'

Wang Bin did not even want to imagine what *that* meant. He only wanted to get out of this awkward predicament he found himself in.

'You can't threaten me. I'll report you to the local Party

Secretariat.'

There was more confidence in his voice. Chief Han was surprised. He had been expecting him to crumble at the mention of legal proceedings. So the Beijinger had some fire in his belly after all. He liked that. He was constantly surrounded by fawning wimps. This guy was going to put up a fight. He would enjoy playing with him, even though it would make him late for Da Jie Jie's.

'Oh yes, Comrade. Perhaps I can call the Party Secretariat for you?'

Chief Han picked up the black phone on his desk and pressed the intercom button.

'Liao. Get the Party Secretary on the line for me.'

He put back the phone and both men waited, one looking pleased, the other amused.

When the phone rang, the Chief passed it to Wang Bin without speaking.

'Party Secretary?'

Wang Bin's nerves made his Beijing accent seem more pronounced.

'Who's this? I was told Chief Han wanted to speak to me.'

'I'm in his office. He kindly got one of his officers to get through to you. My name's Wang Bin.'

'Put me on to Chief Han right now.'

Wang Bin passed the phone to the Chief.

'How goes it, Lao Zhang? ... Yes, I have a guest in my office from Beijing ... He'd like a word with you ... And I'll be a bit late this evening at Da Jie Jie's ... Start without me.'

He handed the phone back to Wang Bin.

'Party Secretary Zhang. I really am sorry to disturb you like this. I've just arrived in Pingyang and I'm in a bit of a fix ... No, I don't know anyone in Beijing who knows you ... Chief Han said I could call you ... No, you see I ... But I've been accused of ... Could I just ...'

Wang Bin was left holding the phone. Utterly deflated.

Chief Han leaned across, gently took it from his hand and put it back in the receiver on his desk.

'As I was saying, I'm your only hope.'

'Please believe me, Chief Han.'

'You've broken the law.'

'But I didn't mean to do anything wrong.'

'Then why the bird in the bag?'

'I've told you I was going to set it free.'

'When?'

'Tomorrow. In the mountains. Where it's less likely to

be caught again.'

'Why not now? There's the river outside that window.'

He pointed to the window behind the settee at the other end of the room.

'OK then. Now.'

Wang Bin stood up and reached for the hemp sack.

'Not so fast. That's evidence you know.'

'Evidence?'

'The judge will want to see it.'

'Judge?'

'The bird's still alive so the sentence probably won't be too severe.'

'Sentence?'

'I reckon two, three years at the most.'

'Please help me, Chief Han. Please help me escape from this place.'

He looked up at the Chief and as they stared into each other's eyes he realized the Chief would help if the price was right.

'No one knows you're here?' There was a secretive tone to the Chief's voice.

'Only the people at the Merchants Hotel.'

The Chief waved his hand to show that would not pose

a problem.

'And the restaurant owner.'

'Li Hai Shan's almost as guilty as you.'

'And your men, I mean officers.'

The Chief merely raised his eyebrows.

'So you could leave tomorrow without any fuss and no one would be the wiser.'

He spoke the words as if thinking out loud.

'How much have you got in your pouch there?'

'A little over four thousand.'

'Let's see it.'

By now, drawn into the conspiratorial mood of the conversation, and only intent on securing a means of escape, Wang Bin was wholeheartedly co-operative. He placed his pouch on the desk and pulled out the wad of one-hundred-yuan notes. Chief Han picked up the money, peeled off two notes, and put the remainder in the inside pocket of his jacket. There was a gold pocket watch and chain, too. Chief Han, without touching the watch, left it where it was, tucked away in the folded pouch, and placed it ever so carefully in the top drawer of his desk.

He handed Wang Bin the two hundred-yuan notes.

'You'll need something for your bus fare back to Beijing.'

'Thank you.'

'Pity about your camera stuff too.'

The Chief picked up the camera bag and placed it on the desk next to the phone.

Wang Bin was about to protest but did not.

'And now, before I get Officer Liao to see you out, what about the bird.'

He picked up the hemp sack and handed it to Wang Bin.

'You said you wanted to set it free. Go on then.'

He nodded towards the window.

6

When Xiao Zhou came out of the police headquarters by Martyrs Bridge she crossed the road to where the long row of small restaurants was and found one with an empty table outside. She could sit there and keep an eye on the gates of the building she had just left. When they released Wang Bin she was sure they would leave him to walk back to the hotel.

She often came to this part of town to unwind after work. She knew most of the restaurant owners and had eaten in every one of the restaurants at some time or other over the years. Now and then her old classmates from Pingyang Middle School would meet up to share a meal and gossip about their boyfriends. The most popular dining spot for them this summer was the one on the corner by the crossroads. She did not walk back down to the crossroads, though, to see if any of her friends were there this evening.

A fly crawled across the table examining the traces left behind after the last wiping.

The restaurant owner poured some more boiling water into Xiao Zhou's glass of tea. The leaves swirled and settled.

'You want to order yet?'

'No. I'll wait for my friend.'

The single sheet menu lay where she had put it, face up on the table.

After a while the restaurant owner came out again and put a small dish of deep fried pieces of pork fat in front of her.

'On the house.'

He did not want her to wander off down the street to another restaurant in search of her friend. The tea was free too.

She nearly missed Wang Bin. Suddenly there he was, about to cross the road to where she was sitting. She got up and went to greet him.

'Hello, Mr Wang. I was hoping to meet you here.'

He did not register who she was. He looked shaken.

'Are you all right? Come and have some tea.'

Xiao Zhou was surprised at her own forwardness. She was glad none of her classmates was there to witness it.

'Oh. It's you.'

He let himself be guided to the table Xiao Zhou had been sitting at. She sat as before facing the street, he, the restaurant. The owner was immediately there with a new glass. The dry tea leaves barely covered the bottom. Boiling water soon made them dance.

'I was waiting for you to come out. I went in and tried to speak to Chief Han about you but he more or less told me to mind my own business. What happened?'

'Is he a friend of yours?'

'Not on your life.'

Wang Bin took a sip of tea. Xiao Zhou waited to hear what he had to say.

'I've been a bloody fool,' he began. 'I should never have come here on my own. Without an introduction from the Ornithological Society. Now look at the mess I've got myself into.'

'Can't I help in any way?'

He proceeded to tell Xiao Zhou what had happened since he left the hotel. She listened, not interrupting him once.

'And so now I'll be taking the first bus back to Chongqing tomorrow morning and from there, back home to Beijing.'

'You've gone and got yourself on the wrong side of Chief Han,' she said at last. 'It all started when you upset Manager Wu. Chief Han stopped by the hotel just after you left and I heard Manager Wu complaining to him about you. They went through your things in the room. Don't let Chief Han trap you into trusting him. He's quite capable of having you arrested again. Just as you're getting on the bus tomorrow.'

'Why would he want to do that? He's already got my money and my camera stuff.'

'Just so that you'll never want to come back here again.'

'He's already made sure of that.'

'And so that you won't have second thoughts once you're back in Beijing. Won't try and make some complaint or other.'

They both fell silent.

Then Wang Bin said, 'How can you live here.' It was not spoken as a question.

Another silence.

'Let's have something to eat. I'll pay. Pingyang's not as bad as all that. If you need some money for the trip back I can lend you a little. Send it back to me later. No hurry if you're a bit short right now. I'm sorry you ended up being robbed.'

'I've still got a thousand hidden in the bottom of my bag back at the hotel. For an emergency. Don't suppose they found it.'

'Why carry so much with you?'

'Thought I might have to hire a four-wheel drive to get up into the mountains, so I borrowed enough from my friends just in case.'

'Chief Han's a real bastard.'

She persuaded him to try a fish hotpot and selected two medium-sized catfish from one of the plastic bowls outside the restaurant entrance. She ordered, too, a dish of mountain vegetables, fried with thick slithers of garlic and ginger, and a plate of thinly sliced, air-dried wild boar, sprinkled with liberal amounts of finely ground chilli powder. Another plate appeared with large red radishes, cut into cubes and pickled overnight. These were tossed in an oily dressing of chilli, salt and monosodium glutamate.

'I hope you like our local food.'

She said this as an afterthought when the dishes were all on the table.

Just then Chief Han's Mitsubishi jeep swept out of the police headquarters and turned left towards the crossroads. The Chief was alone as usual. As he passed by the restaurant where Xiao Zhou and Wang Bin were sitting, he looked straight at Xiao Zhou. She hoped he had not recognized Wang Bin who had his back to the road.

'I don't think he saw you.'

'Who?'

'Chief Han's just driven past. On his way to Da Jie Jie's, no doubt.'

During the meal, she told him about her life in Pingyang, her parents, her friends. What it was like in winter when the snow was so thick you had to shovel it off the roof.

He told her about his modest job as a high school biology teacher, his aspirations to become a famous ornithologist. How hard it was in Beijing to break into the inner circle of the society, despite his impressive university qualifications.

She felt herself blush as she asked him if his girlfriend had the same interests. And buried her nose in her glass of tea as he told her matter-of-factly that there was not anyone special in his life at the moment.

As the meal progressed, they turned their attention to the more immediate problem of his escape from Pingyang.

'I don't think you should take the bus. I think you should get out as quick as you can.'

'Great. But I can't fly.'

She thought a moment.

'I have a friend ... Lao Shi ... Well he's a friend of my parents really. He drives a truck. But not to Chongqing. He goes over the mountains to Changsha. I saw him this morning on my way to work so I know he's in town. Chief Han would never imagine your taking another route out of Pingyang.'

The idea of going to the place where Mao had studied as a young man was tempting, even though it meant a considerable detour.

'Yeah. But I need to leave tonight if I'm to slip through Chief Han's net.'

'I only know he drives overnight to avoid the traffic. But as to whether he's driving out tonight ...' She finished her sentence with a shrug.

'Where can we find him?'

'We'll drop in at his house on the way back to the hotel.'

Wang Bin looked at Xiao Zhou, as if for the first time.

'Xiao Zhou. You're very kind. Why are you helping me?'

'Honestly I don't know. But I do know that I don't like Chief Han and that's reason enough for me.'

She paid for their meal and led Wang Bin down the street towards the crossroads. Before they had walked very far, they ducked into a narrow passage he had not noticed when he first passed that way, and continued through a maze of small alleys, always in the general direction of the main street, until they came to Lao Shi's house.

This part of town, so close to the main thoroughfares, was a lot less clean. Small piles of rubbish accumulated in the alleys outside the entrances to the houses, waiting to be removed. The houses were built in long rows on either side, following the contours of the alleyways. During daylight hours the front doors would be left open and old folk would sit outside on bamboo chairs right in the alley itself; grandmothers unravelling old pullovers and knitting new ones with the balls of wool they had saved; grandfathers smoking hand rolled cigarettes stuck upright in the end of thin brass pipes with long bone stems. Neighbours sometimes chatted. Through the doors you could see into each residence: dark corridors leading to an inner courtyard with more living quarters behind, jutting out over the river or, in this season, the riverbed.

After night fell, lamps would be lit inside. The rows of houses glowed behind their closed windows. Shadows played on the curtains when someone moved inside. A television blared in every front room.

In winter, planks of wood, each with a number on it written in chalk, would be placed one next to the other over the windows to shut out the cold. The alley was quieter then. The noises from inside muffled. In any season, a door might open and a bowl of dirty water, left over from washing cabbages or aching feet, be emptied with a splash onto the cobblestones outside. They were always muddy.

Xiao Zhou knocked on Lao Shi's window and called his name. His wife opened the door and beamed a welcome.

'Come in. Come in. I was only saying to your mother this morning in the market we don't see so much of you now that you're a big girl.'

Xiao Zhou made brief introductions and she and Wang Bin were shuffled into the front room and guided like two stray chicks under the wing of a mother hen to the old worn sofa next to the television. Lao Shi's wife then busied herself with boiling some water and filling the thermos for their tea.

'Don't bother about us. We've just finished eating. We really came to see if Uncle Shi was in.'

'I was just going to wake him. He's driving off to Changsha tonight and hasn't eaten yet. Serves him right for not having his sleep earlier but he would insist on mending his pigeon coop at the back.'

She disappeared down the corridor to the rear of the house.

'Looks as if you're in luck,' Xiao Zhou said.

'My luck seems to be changing at any rate.'

She was quite at home in Lao Shi's house and wondered why indeed she visited them less frequently now that she was working.

Soon Lao Shi appeared, pushed from behind by his wife. He was a big man with tousled hair and a face that beamed with joviality. Next to him his wife seemed so tiny.

'Ah so you've finally come to see if your old friend's still alive.' He broke into a loud laugh. Nothing he ever said was meant to be taken seriously. This at times had its inconveniences. But today he was very happy to see Xiao Zhou.

'You've found a young man at last have you?'

His attention had turned to Wang Bin.

'No wonder you haven't had time to come and visit us.'

He laughed again, sat in his armchair and slapped Wang Bin on the knee.

Xiao Zhou intervened quickly: 'Wang Bin's a friend from Beijing. You remember Pu Lan from middle school. She went there to study a few years ago. Wang Bin's passing through. I thought you wouldn't mind giving him a lift to Changsha. Save him some bus fare.'

'Sure. But I'm leaving in an hour.'

'That suits him fine. Doesn't it,' she added turning now to Wang Bin.

'It's very kind of you, Mr Shi. I can be ready to leave as soon as you like. Shall I get my stuff together and come back to meet you here?'

'No,' interrupted Xiao Zhou. 'I'll take you directly to Uncle Shi's truck. It'll save time.'

Then, turning to Lao Shi. 'You still park the truck behind the bus station, don't you?'

The bus station was on the other side of the hotel. She had not worked out yet how to get Wang Bin's belongings out of his room without being seen.

'Yes. Same old place. Have some tea though before rushing off.'

'No. We'd better go. You'll have plenty of time to get to know Wang Bin on the road. And I promise to come and visit as soon as you're back. Thanks for everything, now.'

She and Wang Bin stood up and made for the door just as Lao Shi's wife came in with a plate of apples she had peeled in the kitchen.

'What's all the hurry, now.'

'Wang Bin's got a ride in Uncle Shi's truck. He's got to get ready. Promise not to leave before we get there.'

'If you say you're coming I'll wait.'

They were through the door in no time and walking briskly down the alley in the direction of the hotel.

7

As soon as Xiao Zhou and Wang Bin were back in the alley he asked her who Pu Lan was.

'Just someone I went to school with. She went to Beijing to continue her studies. Must be three years ago already.'

'You told Lao Shi I knew her.'

'No I didn't. I said you were a friend from Beijing and then I asked him if he remembered Pu Lan.'

She stopped. There happened to be a street lamp just there. She pulled out a notebook and pen from her pocket and started writing the name of the college Pu Lan was studying at.

'Look her up when you get back. She's a nice girl. Studying to be a nurse. Maybe it's a way for us to keep in touch too.'

She felt herself blushing again as she tore out the page and handed it to him, and was glad when they moved on, away from the light cast by the street lamp.

'When we reach the hotel, we don't want anyone to see you. We'll have to sneak in through the back entrance to the courtyard. You didn't leave your room window open by any chance? Never mind. We'll think of something when we get there. But there isn't much time.'

'Can't you get the room key from the reception desk?'

'Not without making Manager Wu suspicious. He's got a nose for anything unusual, that one. Don't forget it's my day off tomorrow. I'm not expected anywhere near the hotel till Friday morning.'

'We can always break the window to get in,' he said at last. 'It looked to me as if someone had done that before, too.'

They walked on in silence, she leading him deftly through the maze of alleyways. Then they suddenly emerged into the main road and he could see the Merchants Hotel on the other side, farther down to their right.

There was still quite a lot of traffic at this time of the evening. They waited for a gap in the steady stream of passing vehicles. Once on the other side, she led him down a lane running along the side of the hotel and through the staff entrance gate into the hotel compound.

It was quieter there. The traffic noise was replaced by muffled sounds from within the hotel buildings: the kitchen, the dining section beyond.

They waited to assess the situation. Two convicts planning an escape. One for good. The accomplice hoping there would be no implicating circumstances, no reprisals, no revenge when the Chief discovered his bird had flown.

Manager Wu was in a foul mood again. Because Wang Bin had not returned to the hotel for dinner, he had not had an excuse to telephone Chief Han and tell him their pigeon was back. Had things been otherwise, Chief Han might even have changed his mind and asked him to join the party at Da Jie Jie's.

And then, on top of everything, he had had an argument with one of the cooks and the service in the restaurant was now even slower than usual.

Locals liked to go there for a Sichuan hotpot. He had increased the number of tables with a gas cylinder fitted out under each and his evening clientele had grown. Now he was short-staffed in the kitchens and he, himself, had his hands full supervising the restaurant service staff and the cashier. Tonight there were more diners than usual. He would not have had time to go to the party at Da Jie Jie's anyway.

Another plate crashed onto the floor tiles in the kitchen.

No sooner had Manager Wu made for the kitchen swing doors to find out which oaf was responsible than there was another smash of glass from within the restaurant. One of the guests had reached for a dish and knocked his glass of beer off the table.

A waitress moved to clear up the mess.

'Put that on his bill,' Manager Wu said as the girl passed in front of him.

Xiao Zhou whispered hoarsely: 'There's a rowdy bunch tonight. We're in luck. Wait here.'

Wang Bin was amazed at the speed at which Xiao Zhou crossed the courtyard. She knew exactly which window was his, and before he had a chance to anticipate her action, she picked up a stone and smashed it. Then she ducked back into the shadows where she had left him. They waited. A noisy argument broke out in the kitchen. Manager Wu was accusing the kitchen staff of negligence and connivance.

Now pans crashed to the floor. Noisily.

Xiao Zhou and Wang Bin sheltered in the shadows between the parked cars as they crept back across the courtyard to the broken window. Xiao Zhou unhooked the latch on the inside and swung it open. A loose piece of glass fell to the concrete parameter outside the room. Another tinkle. Lost in the noise of the argument vibrating from the kitchen.

Wang Bin helped Xiao Zhou climb into the room, then followed, himself.

Yu Mei sat behind the reception desk, perched on a high stool. She could have been sitting at a bar counter except that she was engrossed in re-doing her nails rather than twiddling a cherry in her cocktail.

One of her regulars, a traveling salesman, had given her a sample from his suitcase. He had said it was French.

Manager Wu had gone in to the restaurant section and now she did not have anyone to talk to. He liked to come and talk to her behind the counter when she was on duty by herself and when they were not too busy. Sometimes, when business was really quiet he would call her into his office and shut the door. Most times, though, he came out to the reception desk and leant across her to look at the guest register. He liked her to sit on the stool. She had a habit of wearing skirts with a slit up the side. There was a horizontal expanse of thigh. Just at the right level. She felt the heat of his crotch against her flesh. She liked that, too. Even if Manager Wu was not much to look at. He had plenty of ginger in him. She liked to press her thigh back against him, and think about her handsome traveling salesman, who unfortunately only came through once a week.

Once they were inside the room, they were careful not to switch the light on. By then their eyes had become accustomed to the dark and Wang Bin went straight to where he had left his bag. A quick fumble confirmed it was still locked, as he had left it.

'My toilet kit's in the bathroom. And I have to have a pee,' he said.

'Hurry up, then. And close the door if you have to turn on the light.'

Above the washbasin, the silver coating on the back of the mirror was missing in places, around the edges, a slow decay gradually working its way inwards. It had formed a pattern vaguely reminiscent of the map of China. Beijing was the only really clear patch. Wang Bin polished it with the cuff of his shirtsleeve after splashing some water over his face.

Chief Han felt pleased with himself. He sank back into the soft cushions of one of the armchairs in Da Jie Jie's plushest karaoke room. Everyone in the small room applauded enthusiastically as he put the cordless microphone back on the table in front of him. His hand, now free, drifted back to the knee of the girl perched on the arm of his chair.

He had earlier phoned for a few of the girls from the barber's shop to come round after he and his friends had finished eating. To serve drinks and tidbits.

His party, including himself, comprised the six men he considered the town's elite. Men he needed to keep in his inner circle of friends in order to ensure everything in Pingyang ran smoothly.

Da Jie Jie had served a sumptuous meal, piling plate upon plate on the table. As always, they were only expected to eat a tiny portion of the whole. How deeply they chose to dabble in the deserts he had prepared for them was their choice.

None of his guests dared pick up the microphone. They remembered the early days of Chief Han's parties when Kang Jun, the Director of the Brickworks, had fancied himself, and sang, frankly speaking, in a voice that merited being broadcast over the Central Television Network. He now helps his wife sell vegetables in the market.

'Sing another, Chief Han.'

'Yes. Sing 'The Mountain Huntsman'.'

They all knew which songs he liked singing most.

The girl on the arm of his chair leant forward to take a grape from the plate of fruit on the table and manoeuvred it seductively into his mouth. He bit the tip of her finger. Hard enough to make her squeal, but she knew better than to do that and only pouted her lips at the Chief as he ran his tongue over the finger she had wisely left where it was.

'First we play one of my little games,' he said, turning to his guests.

From his inside pocket, he pulled the wad of notes he had confiscated from Wang Bin and peeled off a hundred-yuan bill for each man in the room.

'Select your partners, now. No one is allowed to stand

and none of the girls is allowed to take a bill from anyone other than her partner. Let's see who can hold onto his bill the longest.'

Wang Bin unlocked his bag, stuffed his toilet kit inside, folded the copy of *International Birdwatcher's Digest* and was about to put that in too when he changed his mind and handed it to Xiao Zhou instead.

'It's not much, but please have this. It's the reason I came here in the first place.'

She was taken aback.

'Oh, I ...' was all she said. Then, 'Hurry. Before we're seen.'

They climbed out through the window again and dipped into the shadows between the parked cars. They waited to see if anyone had heard them. The pulse of the hotel had not quickened.

'When we get outside and make our way to Lao Shi's truck, there won't be a chance to say goodbye to you.'

She raised her hand to the back of his head and brushed her lips against his. A spontaneous movement. Without affectation. Then, tugging at Wang Bin's sleeve, she pulled him behind her to the staff entrance gate and they both slipped out.

Lao Shi drove out of the parking lot and down the main street past the Merchants Hotel. Wang Bin sat in the seat next to him. At the crossroads they turned left towards Martyrs Bridge . They passed the row of restaurants where Wang Bin and Xiao Zhou had eaten. Most were closed by now. A few late diners still lingered in some, the owner hovering nearby, waiting to fold the table and stack the chairs. From the rear of the restaurants that had already closed, lights flickered through locked glass doors, as the owners prepared for bed.

The truck climbed the road above the first five arches to the top of the bridge. Wang Bin looked down from his vantage point over the riverbed. Lights in the police headquarters building were still on but Chief Han's office was in darkness.

The truck stammered momentarily at the highest point on the bridge as Lao Shi changed gear, and then started its descent over the remaining two arches towards the fields, mountains and freedom.

Wang Bin remembered his last glimpse of the Mountain

Phoenix as it had flown away across the river after he had released it from the window in Chief Han's office.

His only thought now was that it had all been worth it, for the sake of the bird. Even if no one else in the Ornithological Society ever knew he had held a Mountain Phoenix in his hands and set it free, *he* knew he had saved the bird and in doing so had helped preserve an endangered species.

Who knows, his action tonight might have even saved the species from total extinction. He really was a great ornithologist. A remarkable naturalist. Maybe one day he would even be as famous as the legendary Ben Hadlock.

These thoughts he could not share with Lao Shi. He would not understand the complicated process involved in the preservation of a species. A feeling of contentment settled over him. He pulled it up and around him like a sleeper snuggling into the soft folds of a blanket.

Lao Shi glanced over at him and said, 'You can catch some shut-eye if you want. I've been snoring all afternoon.'

Li Hai Shan sat on a bamboo stool in the courtyard at the back of his restaurant, smoking his pipe. His wife had already gone to bed. A single electric bulb hanging from a wire strung between two wooden beams cast a warm light over the flagstones of the courtyard and made the shadows beyond deeper. The cage that had housed the Mountain Phoenix rested on top of a wooden crate to one side of the yard. Next to it some rusty tins of paint and some brushes soaking in a jam jar. His bicycle was propped against the wall on the other side. Towards the back of the yard crates of empty beer bottles sat dustily, stacked one on top of the other.

He blew out a stream of tobacco smoke, watched it hover then diffuse in the glow of the light. Night insects kept up a high-pitched hum, near yet distant. Some flying ants danced silently with the moths around the bulb.

Li Hai Shan shifted his position on the stool, raised his right leg to place his heel on the edge. He let his outstretched right arm rest limp and relaxed on his knee. Sitting thus, pensive, almost spiritual, he blew another cloud of tobacco smoke. He ended it with a soft whistle. First a single, long, low note. Then three higher notes. Shorter. Sharper. Louder. The last trailing to a whisper.

He slowly, methodically, repeated the operation three times. By the end of the third, there was a fluttering of wings, an ungainly screech.

The prodigal Mountain Phoenix swooped down into the courtyard, alighted on the wooden box and hopped through the open door back home into its cage.

Li Hai Shan stood up, sauntered over to the cage and carefully took the bird out.

'Well, now, my painted lady. You've been splashing about in the river again, I see.'

He held the bird firmly in his left hand while he prised the lids off the rusty tins of paint with the other. Then, with the deft strokes of a master artist, he daubed orange on the breast feathers where the colour had washed off, scarlet on the sweeping head plumes and turquoise on the tail.

After he had put the bird back in its cage and closed the door, he looked at his watch.

'Still time enough to meet up with Chief Han for desert at Da Jie Jie's,' he said, as much to the bird as to himself.

He clicked off the electric light bulb and wheeled his bicycle back through the restaurant to the street outside.

8

August in Beijing. Hot, dry and dusty. So dusty sometimes that women cover their heads with fine gauze nets. As fine as those a bird poacher might use.

After returning to the capital, Wang Bin did not feel like telling anyone about his misadventure in Pingyang. He collected his pet bird, Confucius, from his neighbours, thanked them for looking after it during his absence and presented them with a large packet of sesame biscuits he had bought before boarding the train.

'You've come back early, Wang Laoshu.'

'I've got things to do before term starts.'

They did not need to know any more.

Back in Wang Bin's flat, Confucius cawed a loud welcome-home greeting. He had been very discreet when Wang Bin had collected him from the neighbours but now that they were alone, he hopped around enthusiastically in the cage waiting to be let out.

It was unusual to keep a crow as a pet. Wang Bin had rescued it when it was a fledgling with a damaged wing. It was being mercilessly attacked by the other crows in the park. Aware of its vulnerability they would have killed it had Wang Bin not intervened. When Wang Bin picked it up, it had pecked furiously at his hand, but he had stroked the bird's beak, calmed it down and nestled it in the warmth of his inside jacket pocket. The other crows had perched in the tree above, had looked on menacingly, angry at being deprived of their kill.

Wang Bin had taken the exhausted young bird back to his flat, tended to its wounds and fed it some soft *mantou* soaked in warm milk. Within a fortnight the broken wing had mended and Wang Bin had started calling the bird Confucius. He had used the name initially as a joke in the school staffroom – 'I have to get back to Confucius' – but when he noticed the bird responding to the name, it stuck, and whenever its name was mentioned, Confucius would let out a loud *caw*.

Wang Bin never intended to keep Confucius as a pet. As soon as the bird was strong enough he had tried to release it.

First he had launched it from the window of his seventh floor flat. But it had flown one circle around the block and then returned to the window ledge to tap on the pane with its beak.

Then Wang Bin had taken the bird to the park where he had first found it and thrown it into the air. It had flown to a tall tree and perched there bobbing its head up and down, watching Wang Bin's every move. There followed a brief encounter with a few of the other crows in the park, and a lot of loud cawing while Confucius established his newfound superiority. The other birds soon gave up any idea of attacking him and kept a healthy distance away.

Wang Bin had then left Confucius there and returned to his flat only to find the bird sitting on the window ledge again, waiting to be let in.

Fascinated by the bird's tenacity, he started reading up on the crow genus and learnt some astounding things about the intelligence of the species. He would often enlighten his colleagues at school with trivia he had come across in his research.

'Did you know that in an urban environment, crows have been observed dropping hard-shelled nuts onto a road and then waiting for a bus or lorry to crush them so that they can later swoop down to eat the kernel?'

'If you throw a stone at a crow or destroy its nest, it will watch you, take note of your bicycle and then do a mess on your saddle when you're not around.'

'Crows can count, you know. I've already taught Confucius to do addition and subtraction.'

Most times Wang Bin's little gems of information were met with a hearty laugh. One or two of his fellow teachers came round to see the prodigious bird for themselves and reported their encounter to the other staff members the next day.

'Quite amazing. The ugly black thing fixes you with its beady eyes and seems to know what you're thinking. I hope it hasn't earmarked my bicycle.'

Wang Bin's reputation as the 'bird man' grew in the school and it was perhaps because of this that he had joined the Beijing Ornithological Society.

His other interest was amateur dramatics. Once a week he attended a class downtown and twice a year his group put on a performance for the local community. They were good and took their hobby seriously. They had an excellent teacher, an old fellow, now retired, who had kept up his interest in the traditional art of play-acting all through the turmoil of the past half-century, albeit at times clandestinely.

Teacher Dang had a wonderful voice, was a talented performer and was a naturally gifted teacher to boot. None of the group ever missed a class unless seriously ill or, as was the recent case for Wang Bin, out of town.

So when Wang Bin turned up at class the day following his return to Beijing, he was welcomed with a degree of surprise.

'Xiao Wang,' Teacher Dang beamed, 'I wasn't expecting you till the end of the month.'

Wang Bin was one of his most promising students.

'Welcome back. Today we are practising the art of make-up.'

His students were sitting around a table in the centre of the room. The table was littered with an array of powders and creams, paints and brushes, false beards and traditional opera masks.

Wang Bin pulled up a stool.

Teacher Dang addressed the whole group.

'On stage, under the floodlights, costumes, masks and make-up are deliberately bold and exaggerated, as too are the gestures you will use with your hands, legs and bodies. As too are the facial expressions you must learn. These will help you convey tiny shifts in emotion, so that even the doorman at the back of the hall will understand what's going on on stage.'

Teacher Dang looked at the upturned faces in front of him and was satisfied that they were all paying attention.

'But before you learn to exaggerate your make-up, you must first learn to apply it naturally. If you are playing the role of a king, a maidservant, a general or an old man, you must first learn to make yourself look and feel like a king, a general, a maidservant or an old man. Then you will truly become the part.

And after you have become the part, then you can begin to add the exaggerated touches to your make-up, which will brighten up the stage under the footlights.

First learn to disguise yourselves so convincingly that you could walk down Chang An Avenue and be taken for real. Then learn to turn that newly disguised person into a made-up actor.'

He paused in his flow and looked again from one face to another. His students were far too respectful to disagree with anything he said, but he sensed confusion.

'Why do you think,' he continued, 'it takes an actor so long to get ready for a performance? Because he needs to become the character before he dons the mask.'

'Come. I will turn Xiao Wang into an old man before your very eyes. He will be so imbued with his new personality that he will even walk with a stoop. Watch and then pair up and practise on each other.'

They all watched as Teacher Dang sat on a stool beside Wang Bin, turned back his student's collar and ran his fingers expertly over his forehead, nose and cheeks, reading the bone structure, like a sculptor preparing to model a face from a lump of clay.

He applied some adhesive to a piece of synthetic rubber, which he then wrapped over Wang Bin's lower jaw and neck to produce grooves and furrows and sagging skin around the jowl. He pulled another piece over his head and down to his eyebrows, to give him a wrinkled forehead and receding hairline with some straggly wisps of long grey hair brushed back over the crown and behind the ears. Teacher Dang then set about applying make-up, very discreetly, very convincingly.

The transformation was remarkable. Within half an hour, Wang Bin became a tired old man. The others stared in disbelief. One of the women fidgeted nervously on her stool and then went to sit on the other side of the table where she felt at a more comfortable distance.

'Practise your walk now.'

Teacher Dang held out a knobbly walking stick and Wang Bin obliged by easing himself to his feet and shuffling to the door and back, his shoulders hunched in a permanent stoop. His fellow students applauded enthusiastically.

Back in his flat, under the watchful eye of Confucius, Wang Bin pulled off the pieces of synthetic rubber Teacher Dang had stuck to his neck and forehead. He then set about removing the make-up. His friends in the class had dared him to keep wearing the disguise until he reached home. At the end of the session they had each acquired a make-up kit and were told to practise in front of a mirror before the next lesson a week from then. Wang Bin was tickled pink that no one had paid any attention to him on his way back home from class, not even when he had asked one of his neighbours at the foot of his block which floor Wang Bin lived on.

'Top floor on the left. Don't think he's in though.'

'That's all right. He's expecting me. I'm sure I won't have to wait long.'

Confucius, of course was not fooled by the disguise and hopped about in his cage pecking at the door, expecting to be let out and given the freedom of the flat, as was the case every time Wang Bin returned.

'Maybe I'm going to enjoy August in Beijing after all, Confucius.'

Confucius, uncaged, hopped onto the bag, which Wang Bin had thrown into a corner of the room the day before, and started pecking at the zip.

'There's nothing in there for you.'

But he remembered he had some clothes to wash and went to take them out of the bag.

Emptying the pockets of one of the shirts, he found the small sheet of paper Xiao Zhou had torn from her notebook to scribble down Pu Lan's address at the nursing college. Wang Bin resolved to try to contact her before the end of the summer break as he had promised.

9

Pu Lan sat on her bed in the dormitory of Beijing 24th Municipal Nursing College and once more read the letter she had received that morning from her old classmate in Pingyang.

The air in the room was still and hot. Even the box fan she had bought at the onset of summer did not seem to make much difference. She missed the clean fresh air of her hometown. Had a sudden desire to ramble in the hills on the other side of Martyrs Bridge. Lie under a tree. Watch the leaves swaying above her head. Gaze into the cloudless blue sky beyond.

Letters from Pingyang were rare mid-year. When Lao Yang in the dormitory guardhouse had handed her the neatly addressed envelope, she had feared it was some terrible news from home. Then, with a flush of excitement, she recognized Zhou Jun's handwriting. Her old friend must be writing to say she was coming to visit. After all it was still the summer holiday season.

Each Spring Festival the two friends met up in Pingyang. Pu Lan always extended the same invitation to Zhou Jun to come and see her in Beijing, but she never did. Perhaps this year ...

He's really nice, Pu Lan. Tall, not bad-looking, has a heart of gold. That lump of goose shit, Chief Han, was a real bastard to him. I've given him your address. Keep him warm for me until I get a chance to see him again. But not too warm now ...

Pu Lan laughed again. Just as she had when she first read the letter on her way to class.

So Zhou Jun meets her Mr Right and then straight away lets him fly away, she thought. And then out loud to herself, 'What on earth does she expect me to do about it?'

As if on cue, there was a shout from down the corridor. 'Li Pu Lan! Phone call!'

She jumped up from her bed and walked quickly to the guardhouse. Lao Yang did not like the student nurses receiving calls and had a habit of putting the phone back on the hook if they took anything more than a minute to get to it.

Lao Yang was looking at her watch when Pu Lan arrived. She narrowed her eyes. Behind her an old dented kettle, blackened by years of use, sat perched on a charcoal burner.

'New boyfriend is it? No idle chit-chat now. Can't have you blocking up the line. There are other people in the dormitory, you know.'

She made sure her voice was just loud enough for the caller at the other end of the line to hear.

'Come on now, Yang Jie. How often do I get calls?'

Lao Yang's face softened. It was true. Li Pu Lan was one of the less troublesome elements in the dormitory. And she always made a point of calling her Yang Jie. Not like some of the names the other students used within earshot behind her back.

'Don't keep the gentleman waiting then.'

'Hello? … Yes, I'm Li Pu Lan … Who's speaking please? … Who? … Oh yes. Hello … Yes, I've just had a letter from her, she said you may be calling … Well, not exactly … How did you get this number?'

The kettle on the charcoal burner at the back of the

room started sending out steam. Lao Yang began fussing with the sheets of newspaper on the table by the phone, getting ready to cut short the telephone communication.

'Look. What's your number? ... Can I call you back in half an hour ... They don't like us using the dormitory phone ... Yes, I'll phone you from outside ... Goodbye for now ...'

She had scribbled down Wang Bin's number on the palm of her hand.

'That's right. Put the blame on me like they all do. Don't like you using the dormitory phone indeed.'

Pu Lan smiled at the woman.

'Well you don't, do you, Yang Jie? Makes you grumpy, doesn't it?'

She hurried back down the corridor towards her room, Lao Yang's voice trailing behind her.

'This isn't the Great Wall Hotel you know ...'

For Lao Yang, the Great Wall Hotel was the epitome of unnecessary foreign extravagance. Although there were many newer and plusher hotels in the capital, the Great Wall had been the first and for her would always represent the beginning of the decay of the old system. She often brought up the hotel's name when she was in a grumpy mood.

Adjusting her red armband she went back into the room to take the kettle off the burner and fill two ancient plastic thermos flasks. One would be for her tea. The other for the bowl she soaked her feet in before turning in for the night.

When Pu Lan first walked past the young man sitting on one of the concrete park benches under a tree, throwing bits of food extracted from a plastic bag to a bunch of big, black, squabbling crows, she never even paused to think he might be Wang Bin. The young man was not sitting, waiting for anyone, and did not look up as she approached. She walked one round of the park but there were only a few old people there at that time of day. The morning *taijichuan* enthusiasts had finished their exercise and gone back to their homes or gone to work.

Beijing 13th municipal park where she had arranged on the phone to meet Wang Bin was not big. She sat on a bench by the lotus pond and waited for him to arrive. As both of them had had something on over the weekend they had agreed that Monday morning would be a good time to meet. Wang Bin's school was still in the middle of the summer vacation and Pu Lan had no classes in her summer course at the nursing college till the late afternoon.

Zhou Jun did not have the dormitory telephone number and had only given Wang Bin the college address. He must be quite resourceful, Pu Lan thought, managing to extract the right dorm number from the college administration. He could not have claimed he was a relative with that Beijing accent of his.

'Are you Li Pu Lan?'

She had not noticed the young man approach. He had finished feeding the crows and clutched the now empty plastic bag in his hand.

She smiled up at him. They shook hands. He sat down beside her.

'I wasn't sure it was you. You didn't seem to be waiting for anyone'

'Neither did you when I walked past just now. I should have guessed, though. Zhou Jun said you liked birds in her letter.' She looked back towards the place where Wang Bin had been feeding the crows. 'Do you really like those things?'

'I didn't use to. Not until I got one as a pet.'

'No kidding? You mean like in a cage?'

'Yes. But most of the time I let him hop and fly about

the room.'

'No.'

'Yep. They're amazingly intelligent and loyal creatures, you know.'

Pu Lan looked back again towards the crows and sneaked a closer look at Wang Bin. Weak chin, but maybe because he was looking down. Untidy hair, but they were meeting outdoors and there was a bit of a breeze. Relaxed. A pleasant enough smile. Zhou Jun said he had a heart of gold. Not the sort of face she would write home about, nor to her best friend away from home. Not her type really. The sort of man you would pass in the park and not look at twice. Which is what she did. The sort of man you would make excuses for. Which is what she was doing now. That was it. He seemed lost. Sort of vague. As if he could not help getting into trouble and then you could not help helping him get out of trouble again. That must be what had attracted Zhou Jun to him.

'You've just come back from Pingyang then? Not a place many people go to on holiday.'

'No, I suppose not.' He was non-committal.

'Zhou Jun didn't write much in her letter. Said that you were a nice person. We should meet. Said that you'd had a run in with Chief Han. We both think he's a bucket of shit, you know.'

'She didn't tell you then?'

Their eyes met. He knew he could trust her. She knew Zhou Jun need have no worries about her keeping him too warm.

'She helped me a lot you know. Without her …'

The hesitation was too long. Pu La could not resist finishing the sentence with the words of a popular song.

' … my life is in the doldrums.' She giggled. Wang Bin did too.

'I'm sorry,' she said. 'I won't interrupt again.'

'Anyway, when I got back, over a week ago now, I felt pretty bad about the whole thing. That's why I didn't contact you immediately. And then I had the devil of a job getting the college to give me your number or even tell me whether or not you were spending the summer in Beijing. The next time I phoned I put on a mountain people's accent, spoke to a nice old biddy, said I was your country cousin visiting the capital for a few days.'

'You can do a mountain people's accent?'

'Win it plisses me. Win I nid to.'

Pu Lan's smiling face broke into an even bigger grin.

Zhou Jun's Prince Charming was turning out to be not bad at all.

'Next to ornithology, my other great hobby is amateur dramatics.'

'You don't say. Zhou Jun didn't mention that in her letter.'

'There wasn't time to tell her much about myself. It all happened so fast.'

Another pause. Awkward this time.

'What happened between you and Chief Han?'

So Wang Bin told her the whole story and Pu Lan listened without once interrupting. She knew all the characters on the stage personally.

Then when he had finished.

'I see. You must feel really sickened. You were lucky to meet Zhou Jun and Lao Shi. And there are other decent folk, too, in Pingyang. A lot of them. They aren't all like Chief Han and his cronies. One day someone will teach the bastard a lesson, and the whole town will set off firecrackers in celebration.'

'That's one of the things I want to talk to you about. I haven't thought of much else since getting back. It's not right that he should get away with things as he does. I have a plan but will need your help.'

'Tell me more.'

'Xiao Zhou told me Chief Han's one weakness is that he is exceedingly superstitious.'

'That's true. He's forever consulting his almanac. Lives by a thousand and one old wives' tales. Keeps talismans everywhere. To protect him from goodness knows what. Claims it's the reason for his success.'

'Then I think my plan will work.'

10

Pu Lan paused on her way up to Wang Bin's flat.

The staircase was dusty and grimy and looked as if it was never cleaned. On each floor landing where the staircase turned to begin the next flight, strings of dried chillies hung from the window. Now and then in the corner there was a pile of onions, leeks, or long Chinese cabbages wilting at the edges. On one floor an old charcoal burner was waiting for the weather to turn cold to be brought inside.

All flats in Beijing were centrally heated. The boilers were turned on without fail on 15th November regardless. If that happened to be a sunny day, you had to remember to leave the windows open to let the heat out, or come back to a suffocating sauna. Most years though the cold spell started before the middle of the month and that was when the charcoal burners came in most useful.

The flats were too small inside to accommodate much.

An overspill into the staircase was almost obligatory. There was no risk of anything left in the common area of the stair landings being stolen. The staircase, though public territory, was considered safe. Residents sometimes carried their bicycles up and propped them there in a corner, with always enough space for residents of the upper floors to pass. They preferred this to leaving their bicycles parked in the courtyard outside the building, where they had been known to be borrowed. Bike thieves were dealt with severely by the authorities. But that still did not stop there being bike thieves. And to lose a bike was a major blow to the pocket as well as the pride.

Although no one believed it likely that anything would be stolen inside the building, in seeming contradiction to this neighbourly trust, each door to each flat was locked and protected by an additional iron grill. Sometimes the residents even installed a solid metal door that would take a would-be thief hours to cut through with a blow torch. This resulted in everyone carrying a heavy bunch of keys around all the time. Getting in in a hurry was no joke. First the padlock key, then the grill key, then each of the two door keys in succession.

As Pu Lan climbed the last flight of stairs she wondered

why anyone would choose to live on the seventh floor without a lift.

She rang Wang Bin's bell. There were some clicks as the double lock inside was turned. The door opened and an old man peered up at her. She thought Wang Bin had said he lived alone.

'Oh. I'm sorry. I thought this was Block 12.'

There was a slight edge of annoyance to her voice. She realized she would be faced with the unwelcome prospect of having to climb yet another seven floors of another block.

'This is Block 12,' said the kindly voice of the old man.

She looked up again at the number on the standard tin plate nailed above the door: 12–7–1. She had not made a mistake after all.

The old man started sorting through a bunch of keys to unlock the grill.

'Does Wang Bin live here?'

'He most certainly does. Come in. Come in.'

He fumbled with the padlock and swung the door open for Pu Lan to enter.

It was a two-roomed flat like many others in that district, originally the property of the factory unit where Wang Bin's father and mother had both worked. Wang Bin's parents had lived there since the flats were built and Wang Bin had grown up there. When the government started selling off state-owned buildings and encouraging the new policy of private ownership, the family had taken advantage of the offer from the factory administration to buy the place. They had pooled their savings and borrowed a little from relatives.

Wang Bin had just graduated from Beijing Normal University when tragedy struck the family. A fire at the factory. A gas explosion. Several of the workers were killed. The accident was reported on national television. There was a hoo-ha about inadequate safety standards. Conservative elements decried China's frantic scramble towards productivity with no concern given to the workers. The Party pointed a finger at the factory leaders, who were promptly disgraced and then replaced. The dead workers were given a memorial service, heroes of the post-Deng era. In front of the press photographers, the local Party Secretary for the precinct shook Wang Bin's hand and presented him with two hastily prepared loyal service medals, and a gold pocket watch on a chain with an inscription on the back: *Long Live Loyalty to the Party*.

Wang Bin now lived alone.

Pu Lan followed the old man in. He smelt vaguely of mothballs in his dark blue jacket buttoned at the collar.

It occurred to her that it was better than smelling of urine, which was what most of the old people she treated on her nursing course smelt of. She walked past the tiny space occupied by the kitchen, noted the door, left ajar, leading to the small squat toilet and makeshift shower, considered a luxury when the flats were built, and on into the living room, where she was expecting to find Wang Bin. Confucius let out a caw and hopped about inside his cage.

'Please take a seat. Can I offer you some tea?'

'No, thank you. I'll wait for Wang Bin.'

'Wait for him to do what?'

'To be here.'

'Oh! I see.'

Neither of them spoke.

Pu Lan let her eyes wander around the room. In one corner there was a plastic-topped table with fold-away legs. It was cluttered with a pile of books and magazines, a small TV and a desk pad, which claimed just enough clear territory on the table-top for writing. The apartment walls were pale blue and in need of a repaint. A poster picture, like the ones you sometimes saw framed in a restaurant, was stuck, unframed, in the middle of the wall opposite the door. The sticky tape securing it to the wall was yellowing and coming away at one corner, together with bits of the pale-blue paint, leaving a white patch of plaster beneath. There were other white patches, too, on the wall, where other pictures must have once been stuck.

It was a photo of a pretty waterfall. There were cherry blossoms in the foreground. Pu Lan thought it must be some place in Japan. Opposite the waterfall picture there was a low cabinet filled with more books and next to that, looking somewhat out of place, was a spanking new hifi set in its own black cabinet with two huge speakers on either side. Whenever Beijingers had a little money they would buy a piece of modern electronic equipment, a TV or a hifi set, before thinking of spending it on redecoration. Confucius' cage was on one of the speakers near the glass-panelled door leading to the tiny, enclosed balcony, which served Wang Bin as a junk room. It was piled high with cardboard boxes thick with dust and looked as if it had not been cleaned for several years, which it had not.

Next to the balcony door there was a single, wooden-framed bed with an old, worn bedspread and two cushions. It was pushed against the wall near the radiator. Pu Lan thought this must be where the old man slept.

She looked at him again. He had a kindly looking face but she imagined he had lived a tough life, seen many changes. The grooves and furrows and sagging skin around the jowl, the wrinkled forehead and receding hairline with some straggly wisps of long grey hair brushed back over the crown and behind the ears, everything about him suggested that he had lived a life of hardship, and that discreetly hidden behind his smile were some grim stories.

'Are you his grandfather?'

'Me? No. But I'm flattered you thought I was.'

Another silence.

'When will he be back?'

'Back where?'

'Back here. When will he be here?'

'But he is here.'

In another situation, sitting in a strange flat with a man she did not know, getting tangential answers to her simple questions, she might have been afraid. But she had experienced the wandering mind of her own grandfather as he grew senile and now transposed her affection to the old man sitting opposite her.

It was her turn to say, 'Oh! I see.' And then in a cajoling

tone and with a twinkle in her eye, 'Well if he's here, where is he?'

The old man eased himself out of his chair, his arm shaking as he put pressure on the walking stick to steady himself. He smiled at Pu Lan, then straightened himself out of his permanent stoop to his full, natural height, placed the walking stick on the table and said in the normal voice of the twenty five-year-old young man he was, 'Did you really not recognize me?'

But Wang Bin had not anticipated Pu Lan's reaction.

She let out a terrified scream. Confucius started cawing noisily, banging the cage with his bill, which only added to the pandemonium.

Wang Bin instinctively stretched out his hands to calm Pu Lan but this only sparked off another louder scream as she jumped up and tried to get behind the chair she had been sitting in.

'Oh for goodness sake. It's me. Wang Bin. This is just actor's make-up.'

And he pulled from his head the wig with its wispy grey hair and synthetic rubber frown lines.

As the rubberised material stretched and gradually split away from the real skin beneath, the kindly old man's features were hideously distorted.

Pu Lan let out an even louder scream and started hyperventilating.

The room began to spin. She let herself be led back to the chair by a now more recognisable Wang Bin and accepted a glass of cold water.

Calmer, but still somewhat short of breath, she looked at Wang Bin and between sips of the water managed to say: 'Don't you ever, ever, play a trick like that on me again.'

'Well I said I was sorry. I really didn't mean to upset you like that. I never imagined ...'

She held up her hand.

'It's alright. It's alright.'

But it clearly was not.

'What on earth possessed you to do something like that anyway? If you were trying to scare the wits out of me you sure succeeded.'

'I wasn't trying anything of the sort. I asked you to come here so I could tell you about the plan. How we can get back at Chief Han. And after your little exhibition, I'm now quite sure he won't recognise me.'

She stared at him in disbelief as realization began to dawn.

'You're not going to ...'

'Yes I am. With a little help from some friends.'

'Let's have that cup of tea shall we?'

Wang Bin had not let on in any way what he had in mind for Chief Han when he first met Pu Lan in the park a few days earlier. That was because he, himself, had not fully worked out what he was going to do. So he had just invited Pu Lan to drop by his flat for a cup of tea, promising that he would tell her about his plan to get back at the nasty chief of police. Pu Lan anyway wanted to meet Confucius, so Wang Bin's flat was an obvious choice of rendezvous.

The idea of getting 'dressed up' for the meeting with her came later. A sort of test, as much for himself as for Pu Lan. If she had recognised him at any point before he revealed his true identity, he would have called the whole thing off. But as it turned out she had been totally taken in by the disguise, and so therefore would Chief Han be.

While Pu Lan listened attentively, Wang Bin elaborated his plan.

11

Xiao Zhou picked up the phone at the reception desk of the Pingyang Merchants Hotel.

'Good morning. This is the Merchants Hotel.'

'Good, it's you. This is Pu Lan.'

'What? Where are you?'

'Act as if I'm a hotel guest phoning in. I don't want Manager Wu to suspect anything.'

'Come on Pu Lan. Quit the funny stuff. Where are you?'

'This is serious, Zhou Jun. Act as if I'm a hotel guest, can't you?'

The tone more than the words made Xiao Zhou realize something was up.

'Yes, sir. Where are you calling from?'

'I'm in Beijing. I phoned twice yesterday. Must have been your day off. I had to hang up twice. Maybe they already suspect something fishy.'

'The line's often difficult to get through on, sir.'

'I wanted to check that you'd got my note. So that you don't think it's some kind of hoax.'

'What note was that, sir?'

'I sent it to your house three days ago. The post office said it would take three days at the most. God, I hope it hasn't gone astray.'

'I'll check this evening, sir. I wouldn't worry. The post office is always very reliable.'

'Look, we're planning to make a trip to Pingyang without anyone knowing.'

'I see, and when will that be for, sir?'

'A week from today. There'll just be the two of us. Me and your Prince Charming.'

'I didn't catch the name, sir.'

'I'm arriving with Wang Bin.'

Xiao Zhou caught her breath.

'I don't think that's a good idea at all, sir.'

'We're not going to stay at the hotel, you bird brain. Get in touch with Uncle Liu and tell him we'll need to hide out at his place for a few days.'

'I understand.'

'Find out from Lao Shi when he's doing his next truck-run to Changsha and tell him we'll meet him there and will want a lift back with him. No one must let on we're arriving. I'll call you again on Monday to check everything's okay.'

'Yes, but …'

'Don't worry, now. I'll explain everything when we meet. Have you got everything now?'

'Yes. That won't be a problem at all, sir.'

'Great. And by the way, Zhou Jun, your boyfriend's real cute and he clearly thinks the same about you. Bye for now.'

Xiao Zhou felt a tingle as she put down the phone. Then she glanced behind her. Manager Wu's office door was closed. He had not heard her answer the call and even if he had he would not have suspected anything, of that she was sure. The phone rang again. It was for a restaurant booking. Manager Wu came out of his office as she was taking down the details. He rubbed his hand over his face, having just woken from a nap.

'Looks as if Saturday's going to be a full house,' he said as he glanced over the booking sheet and then went off in the direction of the kitchens.

He was in a good mood. Xiao Zhou seized her moment.

'I'll need to take this afternoon off to sort out some things at home, if that's all right with you.'

'Sure. But I'll need you on the reception desk on Saturday. I want Yu Mei to help out at the back.'

'If you say so.'

That was typical of Manager Wu. Even when he was in a good mood he never gave anything without immediately expecting a return favour.

A letter was waiting for Xiao Zhou when she reached home. Pu Lan often wrote to her from Beijing so to receive a letter was not anything unusual.

Xiao Zhou, I've met up with your friend, the camera freak from Beijing and I agree he's 'kinda cute'. Congratulations on your 'impeccable taste'. He's a bit weird, too, in a nice way, and very daring. He's told me the story about his clash with Chief Han and how the bastard relieved him of his photographic equipment as well as the contents of his wallet. He's determined to get his own back on him and has come up with a plan to disgrace the man. The scheme's so far-fetched it might just work. I'm more than willing to help him with it if you are, too, and if you can

*rally some support in town. Together we may be able
to give the tyrant his just deserts. This is the plan ...*

When Xiao Zhou received the note, she thought Wang
Bin and Pu Lan had gone mad. The plan was unthinkable.
Living so far away, they had forgotten the suffocating grip
Chief Han had on the town.

'They're nuts,' she said to herself.

She re-read the letter several times, excited by the
audacity of the plan but determined to pick out weaknesses
which she could point out to Wang Bin to deter him from
trying to carry out his scatter-brained idea.

Perhaps it was the confidence in Pu Lan's letter that
gave Xiao Zhou a glimmer of hope. Perhaps her feeling
of helplessness in the face of all the injustices committed
by the Chief gave her the courage to believe in her friend's
optimism. Little by little there was a gentle shift in the
objections she raised in her mind to the plan. Instead of a
total rejection: 'It will never work ...', 'You can't possibly
expect Chief Han to ...', 'You'll never get out of Pingyang
alive ...', she began to add provisos: 'It won't work unless
you ...', 'You'll have to make sure that ...', 'Don't forget
that ...', and then the 'you' changed to 'we': 'We will have to

…', 'We can count on …', 'We're all in this together'.

She put the letter down and gazed up, eyes sparkling with wonderment.

'Yes,' she said out loud. 'The plan'll work. We'll make it work!'

Wang Bin and Pu Lan needed to arrive three days before the full moon. She had ten days to get things ready for them. First things first, she would get Uncle Shi to pick them up in his truck and bring them into town without anyone knowing. Folding the letter carefully and hiding it in her purse, she left for Uncle Shi's home.

'We don't need to give everyone all the details,' said Uncle Shi after Xiao Zhou had shown him the part of the letter outlining the plan. She had kept, folded in the envelope, the first part of the letter where Pu Lan had congratulated her on her 'impeccable taste'. After all, she did not want Uncle Shi jumping to wrong conclusions.

'Why not?' she asked.

'Probably for the same reasons you kept the first part of Pu Lan's letter in the envelope,' he replied. 'We don't want people jumping to wrong conclusions, now, do we?'

He gave her a sideways conspiratorial look. Xiao Zhou blushed, as she always did when he teased her, and Uncle Shi let out a loud guffaw, as *he* always did when he managed to embarrass her in the privacy of their little house.

'I'll let drop the word that the venerable holy man is on his way down from the mountains and we'll arrange a committee to meet him on Martyrs Bridge and the riverbank below. That'll bring traffic to a standstill and there'll be scores of people coming to see what all the commotion is about, including Chief Han himself. You can bet your boots he won't resist a chance to flex his muscles in front of an audience. Then your friend can take it from there. But what does the lad mean about the Chief's Achilles heel? If he had one, he wouldn't be where he is today, would he?'

'I don't know,' Xiao Zhou said. 'I'm going to phone Pu Lan tonight to find out more.'

She felt deflated now. Uncle Shi had immediately identified the vulnerability of the plan. She had rather been hoping instead that he was the one who was going to be able to tell her where there was a chink in the Chief's armour.

'Don't worry,' Uncle Shi continued. 'We'll form an inner circle of people who've been victimised by the bastard. Someone must have some idea about his weak spot. We'll find it and pull him down from his pedestal.'

That evening the two girls spoke over the phone.

'We're all behind you,' Xiao Zhou had said. 'I thought at first you'd flipped but now we're going to make it work. Only one thing worries me. What weak spot are you looking for?'

'Oh. I don't know. Some dark secret. Something only Chief Han himself knows about.'

'Great. How are we going to find that out, short of asking him?'

'There must be something in his past. Some private fear, something he thinks no one knows about. But someone must. See what you can come up with.'

All Xiao Zhou could say to that was, 'I'll do my best,' but her tone betrayed her lack of confidence.

'Come on,' said Pu Lan. 'This scheme's so preposterous it just *has* to work.'

'You're right. See you on Saturday then.'

Xiao Zhou put the phone down and looked up and down the street from the public phone stand to see if anyone had seen her. And what if they had, she thought, they could not possibly imagine what is about to shake this little town up.

The next morning Xiao Zhou went to work as usual. Yu Mei was late, as was her wont, and Xiao Zhou did not think anything of it as she got on with her work at the reception desk. But when Yu Mei did turn up, Xiao Zhou was shocked at the state she was in and immediately went to comfort the girl. Yu Mei had a nasty bloodshot eye and a bruise extending from her right temple to the corner of her lip, which was swollen under the dark red lipstick she had put on in an effort to cover it up.

'Does it notice that much?' Yu Mei said. 'I tried to cover it up with make-up.'

'What on earth did you do?'

'That bastard, Chief Han,' was all she said, and then bit her lip as Xiao Zhou pulled her head to her shoulder in a sisterly hug. Yu Mei was crying now. Xiao Zhou had never seen her cry before. Like this, she seemed so frail, so unlike the self-assured, rather unpleasant and cocky girl she knew.

'Come and sit in the back office for a while. Manager Wu's out of town today. Tell me what happened if it'll make you feel any better.'

It all came out. Yu Mei had gone along to make up the numbers as she often did at one of Chief Han's get-togethers. There had been the usual drinking and the inane games he liked to play, and then, out of the blue, he had given her a vicious backhander across the face in front of everyone.

'It stung like crazy,' she said, 'but I didn't cry. Didn't even move. "That's my girl," he said. "If you'd uttered a sound, I'd've given you one on the other side to match." Then he picked up the bottle and filled his glass again and everyone got back on with the party as if nothing had happened. He didn't say another word to me all evening. I don't give a damn if he crosses me off his list. Good riddance to bad rubbish.'

'The shit bag,' Xiao Zhou said between her teeth.

'Yeah,' Yu Mei said. She was silent for a few moments. 'Don't often hear you say a word like that. Seems to have more force coming from you.'

For the first time since the two girls had met all those months ago, they each felt a new closeness, a complicity of understanding, a sense of mutual support in the face of the unfairness dished out to womanhood by the opposite sex.

'We'll get our own back on him one day,' Xiao Zhou said.

In her role as consoler, she spoke as she had always done whenever she heard of some poor woman being taken advantage of by the Chief. Her reaction was automatic and at the same time resigned. Nothing could be changed. They could only hate silently and commiserate. She had fallen momentarily into the old pattern. Then suddenly she drew back, remembering that they were on the point of changing all that, on the point of dealing Chief Han a blow he would not recover from. She lifted Yu Mei's chin and looked her straight in the eye.

'If you could really get your own back on him, would you?'

The earnest note in her voice made Yu Mei narrow her eyes.

'Like - a - shot,' she said slowly, enunciating each syllable. And then repeated it emphatically. 'Like - a - shot.'

'Well then. Let's do it.'

Xiao Zhou went on to explain the plan to put an end to the tyrant's reign. Yu Mei listened open-eyed. She, who yesterday was the most unlikely of candidates to be co-opted into the inner circle of plotters, was now in the thick of it.

'Thank you. Thank you,' she kept on saying. 'Thank you for giving me this chance. What do you want me to do?'

'You know Chief Han better than I do.'

'You might say that,' Yu Mei said, with a coquettish little smile. She had stopped crying now.

'We need to find a weak point, something in his past that he thinks no one knows about. Has he ever said anything to you that we could use?'

Yu Mei thought.

'Well,' she said, 'we never had any sort of conversation. It was always "Do this, do that" and always in the dark. Always pitch black with the curtains drawn to. He wouldn't ever have the light on. I was always bumping my funny bone on the bedpost. Some of the girls say he even blindfolds them. Makes you feel like you're in a coffin instead of a love nest. You can't imagine just how black pitch black is. That didn't really bother me though. Made it easier for me to imagine I was with my handsome travelling salesman instead of that beak-nosed little brute.'

'But why pitch black? He's not afraid of the light is he? Or maybe of being seen in the light?'

'Wait a minute,' Yu Mei said, with sudden concentration. 'There was once, right at the beginning, when I lost one of my earrings in the bed. A special one that Liang Joon had given me. I had a pen torch in my bag and delved under the sheets while the Chief was sleeping. He's got a number tattooed right on his ...' She paused and looked towards the door of the office, which they had left ajar in case any guest came to the reception desk. Then she leant across and whispered in Xiao Zhou's ear, looking nervously back at the door again.

'No!' said Xiao Zhou.

'Don't ever tell him I told you. He didn't know I'd seen it. He'd kill me if he had an inkling I'd breathed a word to anyone. It was so long ago now, and he was fast asleep. He'd have taken it out on me well before now if he'd known about the pen torch.'

'This might be just what we need,' said Xiao Zhou. 'Don't tell anyone you told me.'

'You must be joking! I'm already beginning to wish I hadn't told *you*.'

'You're sure you've got the number right?'

'Positive. I'm used to remembering long phone numbers. And I made a particular point of remembering the number I saw that night.'

Xiao Zhou started giggling at the thought of Yu Mei fumbling about under the sheet looking for her earring while Chief Han slept.

'Did you find it?' she asked.

'Find what?'

'The earring.'

'Oh yes, I did.'

Yu Mei was giggling, too, now at the memory of that night so long ago.

'I'd better get back to the desk while you slip into your uniform,' Xiao Zhou said at last.

'We'll talk more later.'

12

Uncle Shi squatted on the stool in Kang Jun's kitchen.

'You're a good man and far better off away from Chief Han's inner circle.'

'Aren't we all.'

Kang Jun was a man of few words, but with a great deal of talent. He would have been a good leader and had been earmarked for great things before Chief Han decided to turn on him and pull the rug from under his feet.

The Chief recognized talent and ability and drew such people into his hub of power, succoured them, moulded them to his purpose. But he would not tolerate any threat of competition. He knew Kang Jun could become as powerful a leader as himself and that had to be prevented before he gained too much popularity.

Kang Jun had worked under Chief Han as Deputy Chief of Police for many years before he had been transferred to become Director of the Brickworks. He had remained within the Chief's inner circle after that so that the Chief could monitor his connections and manoeuvre his fall from favour.

'Don't you ever try to sing my song,' he had shouted at him when he had stripped him of rank, privileges and face.

And Kang Jun had been pushed out of the nest. Humbled. Humiliated. But smart enough to bide his time.

'We think there's enough resentment and determination to pull it off. Will you help?'

'What do you want me to do?'

'Fill the vacuum when he's gone. You used to be Deputy Chief of Police. You know the ropes. After you fell out with Chief Han there was a lot of sympathy for you. You've got the trust and respect of the townsfolk.'

'The plan's very ambitious.'

'We need all the help we can get. You used to be very close to him. Where are his weak points?'

'Weak points?' There was bitterness in his voice. 'He has only one weak point. His megalomania. But that's his source of strength, too. He'll make mincemeat of you all.'

'Not if we topple him first.'

'It won't work. Keep out of his way and tell your young

friends they're playing with fire.'

'You won't help then?'

'I certainly won't ...' he paused ' ... hinder your efforts. There is one thing that you may find useful to know. Chief Han keeps all his ill-gotten gains in boxes in the cupboards behind his desk. I saw them once when I interrupted him by mistake in his office. That was while I was still Deputy Chief, shortly before he arranged my transfer. He ties each box up with intricate knots, all different, as if he wants to make sure he knows if anyone's interfered with one of them.'

'That's weird, that is.'

'And there's something else, too. The man's inordinately superstitious. There's a whole bevy of things that make him jump. He won't have anything to do with the number 4 for a start. Then there's ...' Kang Jun went on to list the Chief's superstitious fears, fears that far exceeded the superstitions that average people held. 'The colour white, for example. Have you noticed he never wears it? Won't ever blow his nose on a white tissue? The full moon. Probably because it's white. And clocks, he can't stand clocks. Probably because they're round like the full moon. Won't have a clock in his office nor anywhere else in the police headquarters. How he manages without a wristwatch is anybody's guess.'

'Yeah. And he still knows if you're a minute late when you've been summoned.'

'Uncanny.'

'Uncanny.'

'He thinks it's real unlucky to see a clock, forever reminding you that your time's running out.'

'It's useful to know these things, Kang Jun, but lots of people have similar phobias. Isn't there something that will make him cringe, some private fear that he thinks no one knows about?'

'Nothing makes him cringe. You won't get near enough to see him so much as twitch.'

Uncle Shi looked glum.

'We're not turning back. All I want is a commitment from you that when he's gone you'll be there to stop any of his underlings from trying to usurp power.'

Kang Jun looked long and hard at Uncle Shi.

'Who do you suspect might try something?'

'Most of them are just yes-men without an ounce of leadership ability, but I'm worried about the Party Secretary, Comrade Zhang, and then there's Li Hai Shan with that fake Mountain Phoenix.'

Kang Jun hid his surprise. 'Mmm ... A dark horse that

one. Very few people know about the scam he and Chief Han have been running. How come you're in the picture?'

'I put two and two together after our young friend's visit from Beijing.'

'When's it all going to happen?'

'The eve of the lantern festival.'

'That's next week.'

'I know. That's why we need good people like you in the town on our side.'

'I see you really trust me, Lao Shi. I won't disappoint you. When the time comes, leave Comrade Zhang and Li Hai Shan for me to handle. I promise there'll be no interference from those quarters. And as for filling the vacuum you're worried about ... let's wait and see what the people want.'

Uncle Shi left Kang Jun's house in a more confident mood than when he had arrived.

As soon as he had gone, Kang Jun picked up his mobile phone and dialled a number.

'Comrade Zhang? Something's come up. We need to meet. Usual place. And bring Hai Shan along with you.' He clicked the phone shut.

Chief Han sat at his desk, palms resting on the smooth wood surface and fingers splayed. He looked at the carving of the eagle and the cobra and reached across to run his forefinger first down the bird's beak and then along the snake's head. He liked to sit at his desk, even when there was no one else in the room. This was his place, his seat of power. None of his underlings liked him. He knew that. But they feared him. And that was what mattered. Now he leant across the desk and clutched the two heads, one in each hand. The aggressor and the aggressed, both equally deadly, each equally able to overcome the other. He imagined he felt their power pulsate through his fingers and run up through his outstretched arms like a battery charge. He tensed his body and opened his mouth in silent, tense ecstasy, held the pose a few seconds, then released the two heads and slumped back into the leather softness of his chair.

He swivelled the chair round towards the rows of cupboards behind his desk and unlocked the one nearest to him.

Inside were row upon row of black boxes, each the size and shape of a shoebox, each with a date, a name and an identity card number, his haul of confiscated treasures. There were fancy cameras, rings, gold chains, watches, anything expensive that would not lose its value with age. The watches he wrapped in little black pouches before putting them into the box so that any bad luck they might bring would be imprisoned with them. All the cupboards contained boxes. The dates on the boxes went back for years. He always kept the 'confiscations'. They were his guarantee for a comfortable retirement. They were also his proof of his victims' culpability. Just in case any one of them tried anything funny with their hometown authorities. In the unlikely event of an enquiry, the fact that the evidence of the visitor's crime was there, in police custody, tagged and dated, corroborated the Chief's lily-white innocence of any wrongdoings. No one had ever dared get back at him though. They were all so glad to get off the hook, and by the time he had finished with each of them, they were so scared, they would never think of returning to the scene of the crime.

One woman even wrote a thank you note to Chief Han once she got back to Shanghai.

She probably fancied me, he said to himself. Some women are like that. They see power and authority, and it gives them the hots. They end up begging to submit, begging you to take advantage of them.

But the Chief's golden rule was never to have fun with a tourist. Just a sufficient softening of the authoritative stance to make his victim melt, but never go so far as to lick up the cream. There was enough of that to be had locally without the potential complications that might occur if he helped himself to tourists too.

Chief Han picked up Wang Bin's box, second from the end, and put it on his desk. The pocket watch inside had a particularly loud tick, which momentarily annoyed him. He remembered he had almost thrown it away, with its pathetic inscription on the back, but it was gold, it was evidence, and it would certainly fetch a good price when the time came to sell it.

The camera was worth a lot, too. He patted the lid of the box and chuckled to himself.

'That was a good catch,' he said out loud. 'I thought the lad was going to pee in his pants.'

But the mystery as to how Wang Bin had managed to leave Pingyang without Chief Han knowing eluded him. He felt a tinge of annoyance at the memory of that morning when his plan to toy with the frightened mouse once more had been foiled. The watch inside the box seemed to tick louder. The Chief tried to ignore it by concentrating on the beauty of the knot he had tied to seal the box.

Each of the boxes in the cupboards behind Chief Han's desk was sealed with a different knot. Some beautifully simple, others intriguingly complicated, all waiting for the day Chief Han would leave Pingyang for good with his ill-gotten haul.

He prided himself on being a specialist in tying knots. Long winter months spent as a child cooped up in the snowed-in village they had lived in, with no toys except a length of string to play with, had made Han San Xi an expert in all manner of combinations for tying the ends of the string together. They were a poor family. Their house was just a shack with only one room for them to sleep in. Han San Xi's father would regularly get drunk and come home to beat his mother before forcing himself on her. Whenever his mother knew there was going to be an ugly scene she would hang up a grubby white sheet from two hooks in the ceiling to separate the boy's straw mattress in the corner from the rest of the room. Lying on his back, Han San Xi would hear his father come home, hear his drunken cruelty, hear his mother scream and try to hold back her pain as the bed on the other side of the grubby white sheet urgently creaked and scraped, back and forth, back and forth, on the wooden floorboards. Then, when the violence subsided, he would hear his mother quietly crying on the other side of the grubby white sheet and would sooth himself by tying knots with his length of string. The knots were beautiful, symmetrical, intricate. The patterns he made with the string were a way of removing his pain. Why did she have to sob like that? He was not concerned about her pain. Only his own. The pain he felt as he was forced to listen to her sobs.

There was a small tear in the white sheet. Just big enough for him to look through if he knelt on the straw mattress where he was lying. The first time Han San Xi discovered the tear it was by timid and innocent curiosity that he peeked through the hole to the other side of the room. But it was not long before he began to look forward to watching his parents in their violent acts of fornication. Watching was somehow less painful for him than just listening. He developed a perverted admiration for his father as he watched his mother struggle beneath the weight of his drunken violence. An admiration for his father's display of domination. A strange tingling would run through the child's body and his cheek muscle would twitch and blur the vision of the eye looking through the hole in the sheet.

Then, one night, on the eve of a public holiday to

celebrate the country's national day, San Xi's father caught him peeping through at them ... and turned on the boy in drunken fury.

He dragged him from his hiding place, ripping the sheet from its hooks in the process. It fell over the child like a shroud. While Han San Xi's mother begged her husband not to hurt the child he shoved her violently away and tied his son up in the sheet.

'I'll teach ya not ta snoop,' he said. 'Ya'll remember t'day's date f'ras long as ya live.'

The boy lay motionless listening to his mother's screams. But they were not the same screams as he was used to listening to. These were not screams of pain. They were screams of supplication. There was something unreal, inhuman about the screams. They were ugly. Why did his ugly mother make him listen to her ugly screams, listen to her ugly misery?

And then it happened. He felt first his father's heavy hand pull the sheet back to expose his buttocks. Next his father flipped him over onto his back. He felt the weight of his father's body holding his torso firm and preventing his legs from writhing. Such strength! And then came the red-hot steel needle carving numbers into his flesh.

And through the whiteness of his own screams the boy breathed in an acrid smell, the smell of his father's hate, his mother's misery and his own ecstatic pain.

Comrade Zhang and Li Hai Shan sat in an inconspicuous covered boat moored a hundred yards upstream from Martyrs Bridge . Hai Shan had just boiled a kettle of water on the primus stove and the two friends were sipping tea from their jam-jar mugs.

'He didn't say what it was about?' Hai Shan asked yet again.

'I told you "no", but we'll know soon enough.'

There was a creak on the gangplank connecting the boat to the riverbank, and Kang Jun ducked under the tarpaulin cover and sat down at the low table with his back to the opening, pushing his tea jar forward to be filled with boiling water from the steaming kettle.

'Something's come up,' he then said, 'which none of us was expecting.'

The two men waited for Kang Jun to go on.

'We're not the only ones,' he continued, 'to be plotting a coup.'

He went on to elaborate the daring plan that Lao Shi had unfolded to him earlier that afternoon, and finished by saying, 'Do any of you remember this Wang Bin fellow?'

'I do,' said Hai Shan. 'Very wet behind the ears if you ask me. He won't stand a chance against the Chief.'

'I thought so, too. But at least the Chief won't be expecting anything, so he'll have the element of surprise on his side.'

'But how can he hope to sustain any momentum without the support of the townsfolk.'

'That's where we come in,' said Kang Jun.

Comrade Zhang had remained silent while the two of them were talking, but he now came in with forceful enthusiasm.

'This is the perfect opportunity for us. We should provide all the help and support we can, but if in the end the coup is unsuccessful, we weren't the instigators and we keep our heads and our jobs.'

'What if Chief Han finds out we provided help?' said Hai Shan.

'He won't,' replied Comrade Zhang. 'There'll be such pandemonium that we'll be seen by the Chief as trying to quell the mob rather than inciting it.'

'When's it all going to happen?' asked Hai Shan.

'Next Monday. On the eve of the lantern festival,' said Kang Jun.

'We haven't a minute to lose then.'

'We must each make contact with the cells under our command. Spread the word that something extraordinary's going to happen on Martyrs Bridge before noon on Monday. Get the crowds to gather. Hai Shan, you start getting the street decorated for the lantern festival, and make sure there's a big paper clock on the police headquarters building. Comrade Zhang, contact the Party Secretariat in Changsha and get them to send reinforcements, and just in case they try and get in touch with Chief Han to find out what it's all about, tell Corporal Liao to intercept any calls from Changsha for his boss. Tell him, too, to make sure all the live ammunition is under lock and key. We don't want any stupid accidents.'

13

There was a knock on the door to Chief Han's office. 'What is it?' he called out, annoyed at the interruption, but pleased at the timid subservience of the knock. Just loud enough to catch his attention and yet quiet enough not to disturb him had he been taking a nap.

The door opened and Corporal Liao came into the room.

'Yes,' Chief Han said, in a tone he had perfected over the years. An ambivalent mixture of threat and welcome. The receiver was always caught off balance.

'A spot of trouble, sir. Didn't want to phone through from the front desk in case the others heard. You should be the first to know.'

The Chief narrowed his eyes. Corporal Liao had the makings of a good henchman. He learned fast and was discreet.

'What's up, then?'

'An incident on Martyrs Bridge .'

'Traffic problem?' Corporal Liao was usually assigned to road traffic control when he was not manning the front desk in the headquarters building.

'No. Someone's come in from out of town.'

'Not another photographer!' Chief Han's thoughts wandered to his collection of cameras and photographic equipment in the cupboards behind his desk. He looked at some hard skin on the knuckle of his left hand and started picking at it.

'No. An old man. Some sort of hermit come down from the mountains. He's caused quite a stir. I was going to bring him in but there was a big crowd and they made it clear any police intervention was unwelcome. Didn't want to antagonize them any more than was necessary.'

'A crowd? How many people?'

'I'd say about two hundred, sir.'

Chief Han stopped scrutinizing his knuckle and looked up.

'Two hundred, you say. What were they doing?'

'Just listening to the old man, sir.'

'Some sort of preacher is he?'

'Well, I suppose you might say that, sir.'

'No public gatherings permitted. You know the law. Take some of the men with you and bring him in. He'll soon wish he was back in is cave in the mountains.'

Corporal Liao shifted awkwardly on his feet, but did not leave the room.

'He's some sort of fortune teller, sir. Says he had visions telling him to come down from the mountains and break his oath of silence.'

'You seem to have spent a long time listening to him, Corporal Liao,' sneered the Chief. He got up from behind his desk and walked towards the police officer.

Corporal Liao stood his ground.

'Says he's got a message for you, sir.'

'For me?'

'Well. He says it's for the former Chief Han.'

Chief Han's face turned hard.

'Did you say "former"?'

'No, sir. Not me. It's what he said. So I thought I'd better report the matter to you in person.'

'I'll deal with this matter personally,' hissed the Chief. 'He'll soon find out I'm still alive and kicking.'

And with that he bulldozed his way past Corporal Liao,

through the door and towards the car park.

'Make way. Make way.' Chief Han leant out of the window of his four-wheel drive and shouted at the crowd in between blasts of the jeep's horn.

The crowd moved a modicum. Chief Han was used to everyone jumping to attention in his presence and revved the engine threateningly.

'What's he saying?' said one of the bystanders.

'I can't catch it,' said the man next to him.

Someone in front turned and said, 'The hermit's broken his oath of silence. He's come to warn us about something.'

'What?'

'We'll soon know.'

Realizing the jeep would get no closer, Chief Han got out and pushed his way through the crowd towards the spot where the hermit was standing, at the highest point on the bridge.

Wang Bin was wearing a white robe down to his ankles. Long white hair straggled to his shoulders from the sides of his temples. His head was bald and marked with faint brown age spots. Eyebrows drooped to his high cheekbones making him look like a statue of a learned acolyte in a Buddhist temple. His beard had tinges of yellow and hung, as wispy as his hair, in long threads down to his chest, barely covering a long rosary that drooped around his neck.

His feet were hard and calloused, enclosed in a pair of simple straw sandals he had acquired to complete his get-up down to the last detail.

He leant on a long staff that looked as if it had been polished by years of handling.

The townspeople who were crowded around him were in silent awe. Those further back murmured to each other, asking what words of wisdom the hermit from the mountains had uttered.

Chief Han was exasperated that his presence had been eclipsed by that of the holy man, and pushed his way forward roughly. But the crowd's attention was so riveted on the hermit that people only gave way after they realized it was Chief Han elbowing his way through.

'Watch out for the Chief!'

The whispered word spread forward like a wave breaking on the shore. People's heads turned and a path parted between the Chief and the hermit.

The Chief strode forward now, unhindered, towards his prey.

Wang Bin spoke in a loud voice to the approaching man who was still a good twenty yards away.

'You have done well to come and heed my words. You may still be saved.'

He raised his staff and at that precise moment there was a thundering boom from beyond the hills. People turned their heads towards the mountains.

Pu Lan's timing had been perfect. The dynamite explosion had gone off on cue as Wang Bin gave the signal.

'Theatricals' Wang Bin had said when Pu Lan had choreographed the scene. But she had insisted that it would work.

'The townsfolk need something to jolt them into awareness,' she had said and had got her way.

It had made Chief Han jump, too. And the crowd had seen him jump.

'You're under arrest for disturbing the peace,' growled the Chief. 'Come with me.'

He had not anticipated the crowd's reaction. A few well-placed and well-rehearsed voices now began to call out.

'He's an old man.'

'He hasn't done anything wrong.'

'Leave him alone.'

'Pick on someone your own size'

'He's got nothing for you to steal.'

Chief Han stood face to face with the hermit and looked him straight in the eyes. The Chief's eyes narrowed just enough to make Wang Bin fear he had seen through his cover. But the crowd began booing and the look in the Chief's eyes became hard and spiteful once more. Wang Bin felt the Chief's iron grip on his upper arm.

'We'll soon have you sorted out,' the Chief said.

Wang Bin did not resist and, leaning on his staff, walked steadily beside the Chief as he pushed a way through the crowd to his jeep.

The whiteness of the hermit's robe made the Chief feel uncomfortable. Touching the white sleeve sent a shiver through his body.

Wang Bin sensed this and said, 'I can see you falling into a white abyss.'

'Shut your mouth,' said the Chief over his shoulder. He had moved ahead so as not to feel so close to the whiteness. Now he was pulling the hermit towards the jeep.

'Leave the holy man alone,' shouted a voice in the

crowd. Wang Bin recognized it to be Xiao Zhou's.

'He's done nothing wrong,' a man called out from the throng on the left. Wang Bin could not see him but knew it was Uncle Shi.

'You're asking for trouble if you mess with the soothsayer,' Yu Mei's voice shouted out from somewhere behind them.

'You'll be sorry this time, Comrade Han.' The word 'comrade' was spoken with sarcastic contempt. All these words were now coming spontaneously from the crowd. Wang Bin had no idea who was shouting abuse at the Chief. There were too many voices now. The plan was working beyond their wildest expectations.

By the time they reached the jeep, the crowd was booing loudly. Chief Han pushed Wang Bin roughly into the passenger seat, got behind the steering wheel and slammed his door shut.

Suddenly the crowd fell silent.

Confucius the crow, painted white from beak to tail, landed gracefully, as if from nowhere, onto the roof of the jeep. Two hops later he was above the windscreen and leant over to look directly at Chief Han, who let go of the steering wheel and pushed himself back in his seat as far as he could. Confucius hopped onto the bonnet and eyed his target. Then with tiny hops, a few inches at a time, he came closer to the windscreen.

'Aaah!' The Chief let out a scream. 'Get it away. Get it away.'

The bird stopped in front of the windscreen, leant forward and tapped it loudly, four times, with its beak, its eyes riveted on those of the Chief.

'Aaah!' screamed the Chief once more and fumbled for the ignition as the bird flew up and away.

The crowd parted and he drove back to the police headquarters, blaring his horn non-stop.

At the police headquarters he gestured to Wang Bin to get out and follow him, but then stopped short in front of the main door leading into the building from the front courtyard. A huge clock made out of papier mâché had been fixed on the wall above the door.

'What the hell,' began the Chief. Two police lackeys came running down the steps from the door to help the Chief with his prisoner.

'Who put that bloody thing there?' he shouted pointing at the clock.

One of the young policemen replied. 'They put it up

this morning. It's part of the lantern festival decorations all along the main street.'

'Get it out of my sight,' the Chief roared and strode up the steps to the main door with Wang Bin in tow, hobbling along with his staff.

The two policemen watched in wonderment. Never had they seen the Chief in so little control of himself. Of course they had often seen him in a vindictive rage, but this time he seemed almost frightened of something.

As soon as Wang Bin and Chief Han were in his office, the Chief turned on his prey.

'What's all this crap about a message you're bringing me? What message? Who from?'

Wang Bin stroked his beard and gazed out of the window at the far end of the room.

'You don't mind if I sit down. I've come from afar to see you.'

'What do you mean "to see me"? Do you know who I am?'

'Oh yes,' replied Wang Bin, moving towards the settee by the window with its carved swan's heads as arm rests.

The Chief followed behind. They sat facing each other, Wang Bin with his back to the window.

'Please excuse me,' Wang Bin began. 'I have not spoken for more than forty years.' His voice crackled like an old wireless re-awakened.

It was now the Chief's turn to wait while Wang Bin looked long and hard into his eyes.

'It may already be too late,' he said, not shifting his stare. 'The albino crow has already made an appearance.'

Mention of the bird that had startled the Chief not ten minutes earlier made Chief Han lower his eyes and shift his position on the chair.

'I have a message for you,' said Wang Bin once more.

'What message? Who from?' said the Chief again, but this time his voice had lost its dictatorial edge. There was a note of fear instead.

'It came in a dream, a vision, an insight. These things merge into one up there on the mountain.'

Wang Bin closed his eyes.

'The albino crow was there. It spoke to me'

'You can speak with birds?'

'With this one, yes.'

The Chief's right knee began to bounce up and down, uncontrollably. It had not done that since he had been a teenager. He slapped his hand on it as if it were not part of his body.

'I am to tell you to "undo the knots" and leave town for good before the full moon shines on your sins.'

Chief Han's face was blank

Wang Bin continued, his eyes still closed as if in a trance.

'It will soon be the full moon for the lantern festival. If you leave in time, you may be able to save your life. But the signs are not good. You must act quickly. The clock is ticking.'

Chief Han paled at the mention of a clock, but he shook himself back to the present and there was a hint of his former resilience in the tone of his voice as he said: 'Why do you expect me to believe your nonsense talk?'

'There was also a number, a tattoo of some kind, burnt into human flesh. I didn't understand it. Perhaps you will. I have written it down.'

Then a movement outside the window made the Chief look up. He let out a gasp. Confucius was on the window sill outside, staring in at them.

'Ah! He has come, too,' Wang Bin said, without turning round. 'It may indeed be too late.'

The Chief eased himself sideways out of his chair keeping a wary eye on the window.

Another boom reverberated from the mountains outside. Confucius, as though on cue, tapped four times with his beak on the window pane. The Chief howled like a whipped puppy and moved further away from the window.

'Help me,' he said. 'Please help me. Don't let the bird get me.'

Wang Bin stood and followed him to the centre of the room. Then with a deft few steps to the left, he positioned himself between Chief Han and his desk, with the Chief's back to the window.

'He's come for your soul,' he said, in a matter-of-fact way as if he were talking about someone coming to collect a pile of old newspapers.

'You can talk to it can't you?'

The Chief held on to Wang Bin's robe with both hands, then let go as if he had caught hold of a white-hot poker.

'I'm not ready yet. Help me.'

'Your time's running out. It all depends on you now.'

Keeping a wary distance from the window and the silent, staring crow, Chief Han made a last attempt to dominate the situation and regain his composure.

'You miserable turd,' he hissed at Wang Bin. 'How do I know you're not making this all up. I'll make you sorry you started meddling with me.'

Wang Bin nearly lost his nerve, so forceful was the evil spite in the Chief's eyes, but he kept his eyes riveted on his adversary, and spoke quietly.

'The piece of cloth,' he said at last, 'I must show you the piece of cloth.'

He took a firm grip of Chief Han's arm and sat him in front of the desk while Wang Bin himself moved around to sit in Chief Han's chair. Then from the sleeve of his robe he extracted a folded piece of cloth with a long, neatly drawn number on it, and laid it on the desk in front of Chief Han.

It was as if the Chief had been felled by a single blow. He stared at the number on the piece of cloth in disbelief.

'You can't possibly have …' he was lost for words. If there had been any doubts in the Chief's mind about the authenticity of the hermit and his message, they now vanished.

He was prepared to believe anything Wang Bin told him, to do anything he was asked.

Wang Bin leant forward on the desk and ran his fingers through his beard before speaking again.

'You must undo the knots.'

'Wh … what knots?' stuttered Chief Han.

'You tell me,' said Wang Bin with authority.

There was an apprehensive knock at the door.

'Enter,' Wang Bin called out, and the door opened.

Corporal Liao's chin dropped when he saw Wang Bin sitting in Chief Han's chair, but he pulled himself together and said, 'The crowd outside the building's getting too big. We're not sure what we should do.'

'I'll speak to them,' Wang Bin replied.

The Chief did not turn to look at Corporal Liao. He just sat there with his back to the door, shoulders slumped.

'Is … is everything all right, sir?' Corporal Liao said.

'Quite all right,' Wang Bin replied, before any silence had time to become awkward.

With the thick door to the office open, noises from down the corridor oozed their way into the room. The crowd was becoming more belligerent. They were beginning to chant now.

'Enough's enough! Enough's enough!'

The police officers in the building had never seen anything on this scale before and did not know how to handle it.

'Tell them I'll be out shortly,' said Wang Bin. 'As soon as I've finished speaking with former Chief Han.'

Corporal Liao gave an automatic 'Yes, sir' and backed out of the room closing the door behind him.

Padded silence again.

'They're behind you,' Chief Han said. 'The knots are in the cupboards behind you.'

As if in a trance he took the cupboard keys from his keyring and passed them to Wang Bin.

Wang Bin moved to the cupboards and one by one opened wide each door to reveal the hundreds of boxes Chief Han had kept hidden there, all tied up neatly like parcels ready for posting.

14

Kang Jun made his way through the crowd outside the police headquarters, together with Comrade Zhang and a group from the Party Secretariat and Police Division in Changsha. Comrade Zhang was playing it by ear, ready to tell Chief Han he had anticipated trouble and brought reinforcements to help out, or to hand the Chief over to the armed escort from Changsha

Events moved forward quickly from that moment onwards. As Comrade Zhang and his party ascended the steps to the front door of the building, Wang Bin came out with Chief Han in tow.

The townspeople stopped chanting and stared in amazement at the broken figure of the tyrant who now cowered behind the holy man in white.

Wang Bin raised his arms in a dramatic gesture that Teacher Dang in Beijing would have been proud of.

In a loud voice, which crackled with wisdom and authority, he declared to the crowd outside the police headquarters: 'Chief Han has decided to stand down and relinquish his position as Chief of Police.'

A murmur of disbelief rippled through the crowd. And then Chief Han crumpled to his knees, tears streaming down his face. His voice was that of a small child pleading for mercy.

'Please don't tell Papa. Please don't let Papa hurt me again. Don't let him burn another number. Please.'

His voice pierced the silence and floated into the hearts of the onlookers in a mournful wailing of lost love.

'I didn't mean to do anything bad. Don't let him hurt me again. Please don't let him hurt me again.'

Chief Han was shivering with fear, his body contorted and convulsed.

Wang Bin had to fight against an impulse to kneel beside and comfort the pathetic figure at his feet. But he stood motionless impassively looking down at him. Those witnessing the scene were caught off guard, never had they seen Chief Han like this. The people in the crowd started whispering to each other like a flurry of autumn leaves caught in a gust of wind. Voices were hushed as though they were afraid of being heard. Officers from inside the police headquarters appeared without a sound at the front door of the building to witness the spectacle unfolding outside. Kang Jun and Comrade Zhang, with their escort from Changsha, stopped in their tracks on the steps up to the place where Chief Han cowered. The crowd moved forwards up the stone steps until they formed a semi-circle some four metres in diameter around Wang Bin and Chief Han.

Then, as if on cue, Confucius glided down and came to perch on Wang Bin's shoulder and just at that precise moment the papier mâché clock hanging above the door of the building fell to the ground, bounced once and smashed into small pieces of torn paper and splinters of bamboo. The hour hand came to rest against the police chief's body. He looked down at it, made no attempt to push it aside and, eyes rolling, slumped backwards onto the debris of the clock.

There was a moment of absolute silence and then Pu Lan's nursing instinct made her push her way to the front of the crowd.

'Someone call for an ambulance.'

She knelt beside Chief Han and stretched his twitching body out flat, as she held both his shoulders to the ground like a wrestler pinning down an opponent.

'Quickly! He's having a seizure.'

People started moving. A stretcher appeared from nowhere. Comrade Zhang cleared a path through the crowd and Chief Han was carried by the police contingent from Changsha to one of the waiting ambulances that were already parked around the corner, in anticipation of any untoward eventuality. Yet no one ever had the remotest thought that it would be the Chief who would be using one.

In the ensuing commotion Comrade Zhang told the holy man to go back to his mountain. Wang Bin slipped away while everyone was busy watching what was happening to Chief Han.

And so it was that the hostile crowd, who had been only minutes earlier intent on lynching their hated town tyrant, turned into a compassionate cortege following the ambulance all the way to the hospital, where, upon arrival, Chief Han was pronounced dead.

News of the accident spread quickly and a calmness settled on the little town of Pingyang.

Back in police headquarters, the contingent of party

officials and police officers from Changsha sat sipping tea and smoking in the Chief's office. They felt awkward, as if Chief Han was going to storm into the room at any moment and tell them to put their cigarettes out.

'A tragic ending,' one of the officials said.

'Yes. A real shame,' said Comrade Zhang.

'A lifetime of service to the township,' Kang Jun said. 'We should erect a statue of him outside the building.'

They each took a sip from their jam jars of tea.

'Perhaps not a statue,' Comrade Zhang said. 'Some people might be upset.'

One of the policemen blew a smoke ring.

'A plaque, perhaps.'

No one voiced any sign of agreement or disagreement.

Finally Li Hai Shan said, 'Let's sort out first what to do now. I mean, who's going to be in charge now he's gone?'

The Party Secretary from Changsha turned to Comrade Zhang.

'What's your recommendation, Comrade Zhang?'

'Kang Jun, here, used to be Deputy Chief. He's the obvious choice. At least for now. He knows the ropes.'

They all nodded in agreement and settled back more comfortably at last in their chairs.

Wang Bin, Pu Lan and Xiao Zhou sat silently around the kitchen table in Uncle Shi's house.

'I didn't want him to die,' Wang Bin said.

'No one did,' said Pu Lan.

'Don't any of you go soft on him now,' Uncle Shi interrupted. 'He doesn't deserve any sympathy.'

'But it's as if we killed him,' Xiao Zhou said.

'Don't you ever say that.' Uncle Shi was quick to put things in their proper perspective. 'He got all he deserved. His crimes caught up with him. Remember all the evil he has done to this town.'

They were silent again. A fly settled on the damp cork stopper of the thermos flask at one end of the table. No one paid any attention to it.

Wang Bin spoke.

'Everything seemed to go like clockwork. It was unbelievably easy. And Confucius was amazing.'

Confucius bobbed his head up and down at the mention of his name.

'Whose idea was it to have the papier mâché clock fall to the ground at that precise moment?' Pu Lan asked. 'Brilliant timing.'

They each shrugged a denial of any involvement in that

part of the choreography.

'It must have fallen by itself,' Uncle Shi said. 'Pure luck.'

'Pure fate,' corrected Wang Bin.

A few weeks later back in Beijing, Wang Bin received a registered parcel from Zhang Jun, Pingyang's newly elected Chief of Police. The parcel contained everything that Chief Han had wrongly confiscated from him earlier that summer, together with an official letter of apology for having detained him unnecessarily.

Zhang Jun had untied all the knots and returned all the ill-gotten gains to their rightful owners.

Before Wang Bin and Xiao Zhou's official engagement, he often went to Pingyang to see her and his other friends. Li Hai Shan always asked him to bring Confucius with him. He wanted to introduce the bird to his own painted phoenix, but Wang Bin never took his pet crow to Pingyang again.

During one of his visits, though, he bumped into an amateur photographer staying at the Pingyang Merchants Hotel.

'I've read that there's a rare albino crow living in the mountains around here. I hope I can get a photo of it to send to *International Birdwatcher's Digest*.'

'Oh, I wouldn't believe everything you read,' was Wang Bin's only reply.

More from Monsoon ...

If you enjoyed *The Phoenix and the Crow*, Monsoon has other similar titles that you'll be sure to want to read.

To discover more works of fiction set in Asia, please visit: *www.monsoonbooks.com.sg.*

monsoon

NAZI GORENG

Marco Ferrarese

Nazi Goreng is a disturbing story of one young Malay man's coming-of-age in the big city and offers a stunning portrait of the racial tensions and corruption that pervade Malaysian society. Asrul is a fanatical yet naïve Muslim skinhead from small town Kedah, who finds escape in hardcore punk and aspires to life in the big city. After Asrul is recruited by friend Malik to join a neo-Nazi skinhead gang, the boys move to Penang to realise their racially fuelled teenage dreams.

Petty acts of ethnic violence against immigrant workers and minority groups in the name of Kuasa Melayu (Malay Power) earn Asrul limited social empowerment and occasional ridicule, so it is not without trepidation that he follows Malik again, this time into the seedy world of the Malaysian narcotics trade, where selling drugs offers quick money and street respect. Surrounded by corrupt police officials, shifty Iranians, gun-toting Nigerians and a sexy drug mule from mainland China, Asrul soon finds himself drawn into a downward spiral that makes him question his friends, his loved ones and his core beliefs.

In this intense and gripping debut, Marco Ferrarese dishes up a powerful portrayal of displaced urban Malay life and a culture of corruption and racism that exists in presnt-day Malaysia.

Nazi Goreng has been banned for sale in Malaysia by the Malaysian authorities.

SINGAPORE BLACK

William L. Gibson

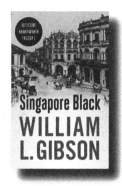

Singapore/Malaya, 1892: When a dead American is found floating in Rochor Canal, Chief Detective Inspector David Hawksworth begins an investigation that quickly leads into a labyrinth of deceit and violence in the polyglot steam-cooker of turn-of-the-century Singapore. As Chinese gangs verge on open turf war and powerful commercial enterprises vie for control of the economy, a stolen statue that houses an ancient Hindu goddess becomes the object of a pursuit with a mounting body count, and its seems that everyone is suffering from maniacal erotic nightmares. Will Hawksworth be able to restore order before the colony is tipped into a bloodbath?

Explore the dark underbelly of nineteenth-century Singapore's Chinatown and colonial district in this hard-boiled historical thriller trilogy, comprising *Singapore Black*, *Singapore Yellow* and *Singapore Red*.

THE SHAMAN OF BALI
John Greet

Adam Milan washes up on the coast of Bali after being forced off a yacht at gunpoint by a psychotic captain. He is rescued and taken in by Agung, a Balinese hotel owner and healer. During his recuperation Adam is reported drowned by the media in his native New Zealand and he sees this as an opportunity for a fresh start in life. Assuming a new identity, he works in Agung's hotel but his new life takes a sinister turn when he becomes entangled in a world of cocaine dealers, gambling and prostitution. Adam learns that the hotel has been used as a front for a drug smuggling operation using Japanese tourists as couriers, and when a friend is arrested with ten kilos of cocaine Adam is forced to help him escape from Bali's notorious Krobokon prison, or 'Hotel K'.

The Shaman of Bali is an authentic, gritty novel based on the experiences of the author, John Greet. Greet spent several years managing a beachfront hotel in Bali, he was involved in illicit cockfighting and gambling, he was associated with drug smugglers and he worked with an Indonesian lawyer paying bribes to court judges to secure friends' release from prison. He was eventually arrested on a drug charge and while behind bars was charged with assaulting a prison guard and spent two years in solitary confinement in leg irons. *The Shaman of Bali* is a novel based on his life.

CIGARETTE GIRL

Ratih Kumala

Pak Raja is dying. In his last moments he calls for Jeng Yah, a woman who is not his wife. His three sons, Lebas, Karim and Tegar – heirs to Kretek Djagad Raja, Indonesia's largest clove cigarette empire – are anxious, and their mother burns with jealousy. So begins the brothers' search into the deepest regions of Java for Jeng Yah to fulfil their father's dying wish, and learn the truth about the family's business and its secrets. The brothers meet an old employee and discover the history of Kretek Djagad Raja before it became the number one brand in Indonesia. They also unravel the love story between their father and Jeng Yah, the owner of Kretek Gadis, a rival cigarette brand that was famous in its time.

Cigarette Girl is more than just a love story and the soul-searching journey of three brothers. Set in Java the story takes its readers through a century of Indonesian history, from the Dutch colonial era to the Japanese occupation, the struggle for independence and the rarely discussed bloody coup of 1965 in which half a million Indonesians were killed.